Return

to

Les Jonquières

[Sébastien revient aux « Jonquières »]

Caroline Muntjewerf

~1~

*S*pring in Provence has been much dryer than in previous years and now the surroundings emit an aridness uncommon for the region at this time of year. Grassy fields wave silvery in the brisk, hot breeze. In contrast, the green foliage of the trees on the gentle rolling hillsides, wafts a welcome freshness. Sébastien drives his car through the landscape he remembers well, breathing in the pure country air. His dark, short hair whips up in irascible movements as the warm wind flows through the open car window. He left Paris early this morning. His suitcase with some of his clothing is in the boot. The rest of his belongings, he plans to collect when he has settled back into his house not far from the seaside. His second marriage failed two years earlier and since the separation, his city-existence has, almost imperceptibly, slipped away from him. A yearning for the life he had known in the country had progressively conquered his love for the city as thoughts from his carefree childhood in the mountains, and his adolescence around the horses of his father had flooded his memory. And his marriage to Natalie that was destined to become a happy one, had not fate intervened.

He is certain he can get his training stables back on track. A subtle smile briefly plays around his full lips. The smile evaporates when he remembers that fate, that was the reason why he left this area.

His eyes catch some goats drifting about in the middle of the road and he slows down. The old man shepherding them guides the animals to the side. He raises his hand in greeting and lets Sébastien pass.

'*Bonjour*,' Sébastien says through the open car window and steers the vehicle around the small herd before gathering speed once more. Another bend in the road reveals the small town as it lies there bathing in the sun against the hillside, but he ignores the road that can lead him there.

The last time he visited his parents was when his father turned 74 last year. His conscience sometimes plagues him for not being more considerate towards the elderly couple but he convinced himself long ago that his father was an understanding man. At the turn-off and barely visible for the shrubbery is the old sign to the property that he has neglected for the past twenty years or so. He drives up the dirt road until, to his left, he sees what once was the sand track where the horses used to be trained. It is totally overgrown by tall grass that extends all the way to the wooded area on the other side. To his right, the fields don't look much better. His foot releases the accelerator slightly and he drives on at a slower pace. Ahead, the old farmhouse with its adjacent stables appear in his view, and he slowly drives onto the yard. He opens the car door but before stepping out, he lets his eyes drift along the abandoned property. The solid stone structure still stands placidly and seems to have stood the tests of nature's tempers, but a few stable doors hang by their hinges. Sébastien steps out onto the yard and walks towards one of the stables. The horse's name is still barely visible through the sun-faded sign: *Jeune Homme*. The animal was his favourite horse and a champion in his day. As Sébastien scratches the rotted woodwork, the stable door at last falls from its rotten wooden post to the ground. Sébastien quickly steps aside while the planks create a cloud of dust by his feet. His eyes observe the front yard and the stables that have been empty for so many years now.

He notices the dead leaves that have gathered in corners by outbuildings as he ambles onward to have a look at the fields that border the stables and the house at the back. They appear not much better than the training track. If he had never known how full of horses these fields once were, they could have passed for a slice of wilderness. Sébastien takes a few steps into the high grass letting his hand slide along the tips of it when he stumbles on a hard object. He sweeps the grass aside and bends down to find a smooth rock with a name engraved: *Belle*. His faithful dog, buried here over forty years ago. How he had mourned that beautiful dog. He had felt so distraught that his father had sent him away on a holiday, to get over the loss of his beloved pet.

Sébastien lets go of the tuft of grass, that sweeps back in place, and he straightens his back.

He returns to the yard in front of the house and walks to the kitchen door. Paint is peeling off its sun-bleached post, and some of the small square windows are cracked and broken. When he finds the door is locked, he walks back to his car, gets in and drives off, leaving a cloud of dust trailing behind.

When he passes the forested area at La Fontenelle, Sébastien soon sees the beautiful white mansion, or 'castle' as it is known locally, loom up in front of him. The wide forecourt is empty, and the surroundings seem abandoned, but as Sébastien steps out of his car, the whinnying of horses reaches his ears. Slowly, as if not desiring to disturb the peacefulness, he walks towards a door by the side of the large house. He takes the two steps and finds this kitchen door is not locked. He sees his stepmother with her back turned by the sink, her arms making busy movements. 'Bonjour, Sylvia,' he utters. His stepmother in her familiar energetic way, turns around and her face lights up.

'Sébastien!' she exclaims and rushes towards him, drying her hands on her apron. 'Sébastien,' she says once more as he feels her moist hands on his cheeks. 'Why didn't you let us know?' She places a kiss on his cheek. Sébastien shrugs his shoulders, 'I'm here now. Were you busy?'

Sylvia waves the remark aside. 'Never mind that, I'm just cleaning some old pottery I found in one of the sheds. How have you been?' She motions him to sit down. 'How's Paris?'

Sébastien notices her long hair has faded even more, from its once shiny raven to a lighter shade. He answers her with another question. 'How is Papa?'

'He's fine, in his study.' She looks at him with eyes that beg for an explanation. Even though she's not the woman who gave life to him, she always senses when something is on his mind.

'I've decided to come back, Sylvia,' Sébastien says.

Sylvia's blue eyes show a subtle sign of concern. 'You wouldn't like me to?' Sébastien asks of her.

'No, no!' she objects. 'Of course you should come back when you want to!' She takes him by his arm. 'Come, let's talk to Pierre,' leading him to the hall. 'You might have returned just in time,' she says. 'Only a few days ago your father had an offer for Les Jonquières.'

'What? But, he can't sell it. Can he?'

Sylvia is compelled to contradict him. 'Yes he can. It's still in his name. And since you've hardly shown interest these past twenty years,' she opens the door to Pierre's study, 'we're not getting any younger, and … '

From behind his desk, Pierre lifts his face up towards the two who have just entered. 'Sébastien!' he says, surprised. Sébastien walks towards his father and embraces him. 'How are you, Papa?'

The old man's face relaxes as he lays eyes on the son he doesn't see as often as he would like to. 'Are you staying long?'

Sébastien nods. 'Yes, I will. I want to move back to Les Jonquières.'

Pierre looks him in the face, then slaps him on his shoulder, 'marvellous!' His father gives him another look, a look that makes him feel uncomfortable. 'Papa. Don't tell me you have sold Les Jonquières.'

Pierre's eyes rest on his son's face, then he turns to his desk and whisks a sheet of paper from its surface. 'You have come just in time,' he says. 'I was about to call my solicitor, to arrange this,' and he hands Sébastien the paper. Sébastien's eyes swiftly slide across the lines with possible plans and conditions. 'But why, Papa? Why would you want to sell without letting any of us know first?'

Pierre now realises he might have been somewhat subjective in his decision, thinking neither of his sons would want to move back to Les Jonquières. He raises his hands, 'I thought … I thought with you living in Paris … And admit it! You have said that you never wanted to live at Les Jonquières again after Natalie's death … and as for François, he is definitely not interested.' The two men look at each other as Sylvia stands beside her husband. 'Neither is Cécile,' she says. 'You know she never liked horses.'

Sébastien turns his head and looks out the window. In the yard a few of his father's jockeys are leading some racehorses back to their stables. He had hoped that he could in some way improve the relationship with his estranged daughter Cécile.

'When was the last time you saw her, Sébastien?' he hears Sylvia ask. He turns around; he can't recall when. 'How is she?' he enquires. Sylvia sighs and shakes her head. 'Have you eaten?' she asks. 'Shall I have Jeanette make you something?'

Pierre goes over to his son and places a hand on his shoulder. 'I'm glad you decided to return to Les Jonquières. You belong there. You never belonged in Paris.'

Sébastien relinquishes, his father is right. For more than twenty years he has been running away from situations he would never have been able to change. Sylvia moves in between them and wreathes her arms around her husband and her stepson. 'It's good to have you back,' she says.

The temperature has dropped a few degrees now that the sun has moved on, further west, leaving the Mediterranean behind. There's a stillness in the air when Sébastien strolls by the edge of the forest that borders the fields. A vague moon lights his way, and he hears some of his father's horses shuffling about in the grass.

He was an avid horseman when he was younger, but gradually he lost the love he had for the animals; the peculiar ways destiny plays with people's lives. Sébastien leans on the fence and notices the horses as the moonshine shimmers on their backs. They could never be blamed for his wife's death. It's been almost twenty-five years. One of the horses moves to the fence and pushes his head against Sébastien's hand. He feels the velvet nose of the animal rub his skin. With a habitual movement, Sébastien strokes the animal on his neck. Then, abruptly, he moves away from the fence, and returns to the white mansion that is lit by a few lampposts at the back of the house. He finds his parents sitting on the terrace, drinking a glass of wine. His father looks up at him; he knows he was with the horses. Sébastien takes a seat as Sylvia pours a glass for him as well.

'We have twenty-eight horses at present,' Pierre says. 'Nine are ours, the rest we train for others.'

Sébastien glances at his stepmother. Like his father she, too, always regretted that he had turned his back on what he had always loved. 'Twenty-eight?' Sébastien replies.

Pierre looks at his wife before he addresses Sébastien. 'You know what Natalie always – '

'Papa, please.'

'No son, hear me out. You can't keep running away from that. Natalie had this idea to one day make Les Jonquières a home for ageing racehorses. You know how she loved those animals – '

'The animals killed her,' Sébastien reminds his father.

'You can't keep blaming the horses for that accident, Sébastien,' Sylvia says. 'Your father is right. You should make Les Jonquières a home for retired racehorses, in Natalie's memory. That's what she always wanted.'

Sébastien averts his head. He doesn't like to be reminded of the only love of his life. 'We'll see,' he says and stands up to walk into the house. Sylvia's gaze follows him while her face shows empathy. The wrinkles in Pierre's face intensify, and he rolls his glass of wine between his fingers. 'Sometimes I don't understand him. You'd expect us old folks to be stuck in the past, but when I look at him … '

'Give him time,' Sylvia says.

The following morning Pierre's enraged voice rings through the open window of his study. Stable lads turn their heads in the direction of the office, they're not used to their boss sounding so furious. Sylvia leaves the basket with flowers she cut, and walks into the house where she bumps into her stepson in the hall. He has just come down the stairs, barefooted and wearing only a pair of pyjama pants.

'What's with him?' she wonders.

Sébastien frowns as he continues to the kitchen. 'He's on the phone with that developer.'

'And?'

'Well, it doesn't sound good,' Sébastien ascertains and pours some coffee in a mug. He is late rising this morning. It was his father's angry voice that woke him.

'I can't remember him ever being so cross?' Sylvia remarks as she faces the hall with a surprised look on her face. They hear a harsh thump coming from the study.

'I can,' Sébastien says. A recollection of his troubled, angry father slapping him when he was a child, fleetingly crosses his mind. The old stable hand Thomas was the one who had consoled him then.

The door of the study flies open, and an angry faced Pierre enters the hall. His outrage seems to have aged him a few more years. 'Bastard!' Pierre cries. Sylvia quickly goes to his side and rests a hand on his arm. 'Pierre, please.' Her calming endearment doesn't change his attitude.

'That bastard threatens me with a lawsuit! But he has nothing on me!' Pierre shouts.

Sébastien is surprised. 'A lawsuit? What on earth for?'

'We didn't even sign a contract!' Pierre shouts.

'Papa,' Sébastien says in a calming tone. 'Please,

calm down.' Pierre looks at him, the anger still visible in his eyes. 'He says we had a deal, and that now I've decided not to sell, he claims I've ruined him.'

'Sell what?' Then it dawns on Sébastien. 'Sell Les Jonquières?'

'Yes! What else!'

Sylvia moves her hand along Pierre's back. 'Come, sit down, *chéri*. Mind your heart.' With a heavy sigh Pierre pulls a chair aside and sits down at the table.

'Have you called *monsieur* Ledoux?' Sylvia asks. 'He'll sort the matter.'

Sébastien takes a seat next to his father. 'Papa, he doesn't have a case when there's no contract between the two of you.' Sylvia puts a cup of coffee in front of her husband. 'Sébastien is right. Don't get yourself all worked up over it.'

Pierre's angry face slowly relaxes. 'I can't bear it when people accuse me,' he says. 'And it's not my problem that he's almost bankrupt.'

'Bankrupt?' Sébastien wonders. 'Where was he going to get the money from then, to buy Les Jonquières?'

Pierre sighs. 'He had a deal with a bank. They were going to finance his project, and when all the *luxury* apartments were sold, he'd pay them back,' putting a demeaning emphasis on *luxury*.

'What? Luxury apartments at Les Jonquières?'

'*On* Les Jonquières,' his father corrects him. 'Can you imagine, that beautiful landscape full of apartments for rich people from God knows where?'

Sébastien shakes his head. 'It would have ruined the whole area. But, Papa, you wanted to sell!'

'I didn't know what his plans were!' Pierre defends himself. 'If I'd known, I would never have considered his offer.' He looks down at his coffee cup. 'He lied to me.'

Sylvia rests her hands on her husband's shoulders. 'Thank God Sébastien came back when he did,' she says. 'Now, shall we sit outside before it gets too hot, and have coffee?'

Pierre rises from his chair. 'I'd better call Jean-Luc first,' and he goes back to his study to contact his solicitor. Sébastien gets up and tips the left-over coffee from his mug in the sink. 'I'll have another coffee with you, Sylvia,' he says, 'before I go back to Les Jonquières. To see what I can do there.'

After his inspection of the house at Les Jonquières and a thorough look at the stables and outbuildings, Sébastien drives through the sleepy heat of the afternoon in the direction of the village. He had wound down the car windows, allowing the warm country air to blow through the interior of his Citroën. He'd forgotten how large the property was and he now realises there is much to be done if he is to make it liveable again. Feelings of ambiguity temper with his feelings of determination he only recently felt about returning to this area. He remembers the years in Paris, and how pleasurable and contented they were. The days at the office, the evenings relaxing at local cafes or restaurants with his wife Angéline, and weekends driving through the country side. For years he had deluded himself into believing that he was leading an ideal life. Occasionally, however, his past had gnawed at his conscience whenever he saw a young woman with long auburn hair pass. Sometimes he had joked about Natalie's hair being the same colour as that of her horse's mane. Or when he saw teenagers giggling in coffee shops, which had him wonder how his own daughter had built a life for herself without his guidance. After Natalie's accident, he had left the care of the child to his parents. He had never anticipated *not* returning to Les Jonquières.

All of a sudden, a large white animal emerges in front of his car. Sébastien slams on his brakes and he hears what he perceives to be a loud thump on the left side of his car, that now glides into the shoulder. Sébastien sees the animal limp into the shrubbery. He steps out and glances briefly at the front of his Citroën before he walks to where he saw the animal disappear. His eyes skim the low, dry foliage when he hears a soft whimper. He pushes branches aside as he makes his way through; a thorn scratches his wrist. He then sees the white coat of the animal shimmer through the foliage. Sébastien bends the branches to one side and then looks in the face of a dog, which sends a pang through his heart. The brown eyes of the animal look at him, plead with him. Eyes that he recognises from long ago. 'It's all right,' Sébastien utters softly. He's still trying to comprehend how much the dog looks like the one he had to bury over forty years ago.

'It's all right, boy,' Sébastien says once more as he reaches to stroke the animal's fur. 'Are you OK?' The dog raises another whimper as he looks at Sébastien with his pleading brown eyes. 'I'd better get you out of here,' the latter decides. He shoves his hands underneath the animal, trying to lift him off the ground. 'Boy, you're heavy,' he sighs. With Sébastien attempting to make him move, the dog struggles to his feet, lifting his front right leg. 'Good boy,' Sébastien encourages. 'Come, slowly.' He guides the dog through the shrubs, it limps as it finds his way. By the road side the animal sinks down and looks up at Sébastien who walks over to his car and opens the back door. He then lifts the animal off the dirt. 'You are one heavy dog,' he groans while he carries the animal and manages to lay him down in the back seat. 'Now, you stay quiet back there,' he says as he sits behind the wheel. Sébastien starts the engine and slowly drives back onto the road.

When he has left the forested area behind, the small stone houses of the village soon come into view. Whenever he sees the village, it never fails to impress upon him feelings of its unassuming, grounded nature. As he drives through the town's main street, the dog panting in the back seat, he searches for a sign: *Clinique vétérinaire*. He slows down when he sees two old men sitting on a bench, their hands leaning on their walking sticks. He asks them for directions to the animal clinic. The old men simultaneously lift their furrowed faces up at him, then point their sticks in the onward direction and to a road off the main street, nodding '*à gauche, à gauche.*'

'*Merci,*' Sébastien thanks them and slowly presses the accelerator down. The veterinarian's clinic isn't hard to find, and he parks his car right in front of it. He gets out and opens the backdoor for the dog who, with some help from Sébastien, lands on all threes. He holds up his injured leg, as if to remind his saviour of his injury. 'Can you walk?' Sébastien asks, realising with surprise that he is addressing a creature that can't speak, as if he were human. Old habits die hard, he finds.

The dog limps beside him as Sébastien opens the door. On entering the practice, a short ring from a bell sounds, and a man in his mid-thirties emerges in the doorway opposite. 'Bonjour,' he says, before casting his eyes on the white dog who now wags his tail. Something that tells Sébastien the two must be acquainted. He stretches out his hand to introduce himself.

'Can you have a look at the dog?' Sébastien then asks. 'He ran into my car.'

The veterinarian kneels in front of the dog and holds the animal's head between his hands. 'What have you got yourself into now, old friend?' he wonders.

'Is he your dog?' Sébastien asks. The vet stands up and shakes his head. 'No, he belongs to Michèl Beauchamp. He owns the café, you probably passed it when you entered the village. But Métèque here,' and he pats the dog on his head, 'is everybody's friend. Aren't you, you *vaurien*.' The dog takes it all in his stride. 'He roams all over the area,' the vet informs him.

Sébastien rests his hand on the dog's right shoulder. 'Here's where I hit him.'

The veterinarian palpates the area, the dog pulls back. 'Métèque, stand still,' the vet says with an observing face. He uses his stethoscope for a more accurate judgement as Sébastien watches his movements.

'He's fine. Just a few bruises,' the veterinarian then assesses. 'I'll keep him here for observation, and then the family can come and collect him.'

Sébastien takes another look at the dog and expresses his thanks. '*Bien. Merci beaucoup*. How much do I owe you?'

'Not to worry. I'll sort something with Michèl,' the vet replies, 'and he'll be fine,' he adds, patting the dog on his head.

'I hope he stays out of trouble now,' Sébastien says and walks to the door, leaving the animal in the care of the veterinarian. In the dusty street, he inspects the damage to his car. The left front light has a small crack, and there's a barely visible dent by the side of it. He gets in and drives the car to the café the veterinarian was talking about.

'Café ct Bar Villeneuve' the sign says. As he enters the establishment, a few faces turn in his direction, but he has been away too long to recognise any of them. Sébastien sits down and when a lady comes to take his order, he notices a familiar trait in her face. Recollections of a woman who owned a bakery in the town, enter his mind. 'Bonjour. A glass of wine, monsieur?'

Sébastien shakes his head. '*Non, eau minérale.* With a slice of lemon, please.' He watches her walk back to the counter to collect the order. His glance drifts around the room. A few middle-aged men are having their afternoon tipples. When the lady returns with his drink, he asks her if she knows of any men in the town looking for work. The woman shakes her head. 'Not that I know of, but you could ask at the agency.' She looks at him with eyes that harbour mistrust. 'Are you new here, monsieur?'

'Not entirely. I grew up here, I lived here until … until. My name is Sébastien Maréchal.'

The woman's eyes suddenly light up. 'But of course! Everybody knows monsieur et madame Maréchal! And you are their son?'

Sébastien nods affirmatively.

'Welcome, welcome!' the lady expresses. She rushes to the back. 'Michèl! Michèl! Where are you?'

Sébastien hears thundering feet coming down a staircase, and a man enters the café with fright in his face. 'What? What is it, woman?'

'Look,' she says. 'Look who has returned!' She points in the direction of Sébastien who sits sipping his water. The man gazes in his direction. 'Have you gone mad?' he asks the woman. 'He's just a customer!'

'*Mais non*! He is monsieur Maréchal's son! He has returned!'

Michèl throws an inquisitive look his way and quickly walks towards him, 'Monsieur Maréchal,' and grabs Sébastien's hand, 'welcome back.' He has a broad smile on his face that Sébastien returns with a more modest one. He is somewhat embarrassed by the reception. 'Are you Michèl Beauchamp?' he asks. The man nods eagerly.

'Maybe you can tell me if you know of any men who are looking for work in the area.'

'Of course, of course,' is the reply. 'I will ask around for you. Are you really here to stay?'

Sébastien nods. 'You can contact my father if you hear anything.' He takes the last sip of his eau minérale and reaches in his pocket to pay but Michèl pushes his hand away. 'On the house,' he says.

When the coolness of the evening has descended on La Fontenelle Pierre, Sylvia and Sébastien have moved to the terrace to take their evening meal. Birds of the evening are heard all around, and frogs croak in the pond, interspersed by the nickering and whinnying of the horses in the fields around the house. Sébastien realises how much he has missed these simple comforts, which belong there where life has retained its authenticity and charm.

'Yes,' Pierre says and takes a sip from his glass, 'news travels fast in this region. There's no need for all that *jouets internet* here.' Sylvia throws a jocular smile his way. Sébastien had made them part of his experiences in the café that afternoon.

'Of course, they knew that I was thinking of selling Les Jonquières,' Pierre continues between two bites. 'And that made them afraid, naturally, when Jonquières had ended up in the hands of strangers. You can't foresee what you bring into the area. No one from here would have been able to buy the property. They just don't have the money.' He looks up from his plate to face Sébastien. 'No wonder you were welcomed so warmly.'

Sylvia places a hand on her stepson's arm. Pierre's eyes remain focused on Sébastien's face, eyes that tell the latter all is not yet said. 'Cécile phoned us this afternoon when you were out,' Pierre continues. 'When I told her you were here, she didn't want to talk to us any longer.'

Sylvia averts her eyes as Pierre looks at Sébastien. Pierre himself had been absent from Sébastien's life the first nine years of *his* existence, but afterwards they grew very close.

'I'm sorry, Papa. I wish she wasn't like that.' He moves his fork around his plate where the food now lies untouched.

'You wouldn't be able to tell what she is like, Sébastien. You hardly know her.'

'Papa ... '

Sylvia faces her husband. 'Don't start that again, Pierre. Let's have our dinner in peace.'

Pierre complies. In silence, they continue their meal until Pierre stands up and walks into the house. Sébastien glances at his stepmother.

'He's getting older,' Sylvia says. 'He wants to see you become the father to Cécile you always should have been.' Sébastien sighs and rises from his chair. He walks into the garden and strolls in the direction of the stable blocks. Not all the horses are outside, and in one of the stables he notices Jeune Homme, who by now has aged and hasn't raced in years.

Under the glow of a lamppost in the yard Sébastien observes the animal as he shows his head above the open upper door. 'Jeune Homme,' he says in a soft voice. The horse turns his head his way and lets out a short whicker. Sébastien walks towards him. 'Jeune Homme. You still recognise me?' Again, the horse nickers and pushes his face against Sébastien's shoulder. 'You do, you still know who I am.' He strokes the horse on his neck and he feels elation flow over him. The horse's acknowledgement after all these years gladdens Sébastien in a way he hadn't anticipated. He moves his arms around the neck of his horse and embraces him. 'Jeune Homme,' he repeats once more. 'Not so *jeune* any more, my old friend.'

He opens the lower part of the stable door and walks in. Under the shine from the lights in the stables, he inspects his horse, sliding his hands along the horse's legs while the animal moves his head his way. 'My old friend,' Sébastien expresses. 'Well, we could try. Tomorrow. Maybe you still have some spunk left in you.' His hand slides along the horse's side, and Sébastien begins to walk outside, closing the lower door.

The horse presses his head against Sébastien's chest. '*Oui, mon vieux. Demain.* I will have to change your name now. *Vieil* Homme.' Sébastien feels the animal's muscular yet velvety lips nibble his hand, when he hears footsteps behind him. As he turns around, he sees his father approach. Pierre remains quiet and stands on the other side of Jeune Homme to acknowledge the animal. 'They still ride him every now and then, Sébastien,' he then says, 'but he doesn't have the stamina he used to have.' Sébastien gives his horse another glance and then turns. Pierre follows in his stride and places a hand on his son's shoulder. Together they walk back through the refreshing evening air.

When Sébastien enters the yard at Jonquières the following morning, he glances up in wonder from behind the wheel of his car. Five men are waiting by the stable block. They cheerfully greet him when he steps out of his car. 'You need workmen?' one of them asks. News *does* travel fast here, Sébastien establishes. He walks towards them and starts shaking hands. The man who appears to be the oldest must be about seventy but he looks lean and fit. 'Nicolas,' he introduces himself. The others could all be in their fifties, apart from the one who introduces himself as

Raymond. He doesn't look a day older than forty.

'Julien,' the man with a more pronounced posture says. The last two have foreign sounding names and don't look like they are from the area. 'Leonek. Leo,' one says. The last man introduces himself as Theodore.

The efficiency he was used to in his job in the city compels Sébastien to show the men at once what he wants done. He begins by instructing them to clear the stables of excess material. He then shows them the house. It only has a chair and a long table left in the kitchen. 'This needs cleaning,' he explains. 'Then,' and he walks outside again where the men follow him, 'the fields all around here need mowing, so if any of you know someone who can provide us with the right machines, that would be very welcome.'

The driven way their new '*patron*' is trying to gain momentum in order to bring something back that seemed lost to the area, touches Raymond, Julien and Nicolas. It motivates them to start immediately. The other two men follow them closely.

'I've no confidence in the machines you'll find in the sheds here,' Sébastien adds. 'They haven't been used in years.'

'OK, patron.' They go into the stable block while Sébastien enters the house that was his home for some twenty years of his life. Its present state could wrong-foot certain people but since his return, he remembers the many happy times that took place in this house. A house that was always so full of life. He strolls up the dusty staircase as he had done only the day before. Now, he wants to inspect the rooms upstairs more closely. His father had them all cleared and stored the furniture when it had become evident that his son wasn't coming back. Creaking floorboards accompany him as he makes his way across the landing. Sébastien opens the door of the first bedroom and glances inside; it was his daughter Cécile's. She was only four when she slept here for the last time. He carefully closes the door and wanders across the landing to another room. He takes hold of the doorknob and his hand slowly turns it. The opening door reveals the room he hasn't laid eyes on since he left. It was his and his wife's bedroom. The dry hinges squeak as the door opens wider. Dilatorily, he walks into the room where dust and dirt cover the floor. He observes its emptiness, when he sees something underneath the windowsill. He walks towards it, and as he picks it up dust rises from it. He recognises it as one of Cécile's dolls. His daughter Cécile left a doll in her parents' room. He feels a tightness in his stomach. His dear sweet naughty daughter who never liked horses. How can he ever make amends? How can he ever be the father to her that he always should have been? He stares out the window, trying to recall when he last saw her. It must have been at Angéline's birthday party, just before they split up. It must have been then when he last saw his daughter.

His eyes rest on a figure below in the field.

How old is his Cécile now? Twenty-seven. No, no, she just turned twenty-eight, he remembers.

Sébastien looks more keenly when he sees the man in the field hurl something. Suddenly, flames shoot up between the high grass, and within seconds the dry area all around catches fire. Sébastien rushes out and runs down the stairs, through the kitchen and into the yard.

'Hey! Hey!' he yells. 'Have you men gone insane?!'

One by one the five workmen appear from the stables.

'Who's that guy in the field?' Sébastien demands, astounded. A few men shrug their shoulders. 'What guy?'

'Someone just set the field at the back on fire!'

'*Mon Dieu!*' Alarmed, they rush around the stables and push towards the field at the back. 'The area is dry as dust!'

Someone pulls out his phone and calls a number. Sébastien hurries to the well at the far end of the yard to see if it still holds water. He throws a stone inside it. A splash echoes after seconds that take too long to pass. 'Hey!' he yells at the men. 'Hey! Do we have any buckets here?'

One of the men faces him and shakes his head. He points in the distance where the flames are spreading rapidly. Agitated, Sébastien runs towards them. 'We need to do something! Or we'll have a forest fire on our hands!'

They all agree. 'But, how can we stop it?' Julien calls out.

Sébastien runs towards one of the sheds where he remembers they used to keep hoses and other materials. The door is locked, but Sébastien uses all his strength to open it. He pulls until a plank breaks away from the door and he is able to get in. A quick inspection reveals agricultural machinery and some smaller equipment. He also finds a hose but instantly realises it's pointless because the property hasn't been connected to the mains yet. 'Patron!' he hears someone yell. 'Patron!'

As Sébastien rushes out of the shed and towards the men, he hears the siren from a fire engine. The sound comes closer, and soon they see the vehicle race along the dirt road, around the house and towards the billowing smoke in the field. They stop near the fire. 'Let's hope they have water in that tank,' Sébastien says and strides towards the burning earth as fast as the high grass permits him. By now several square metres are on fire. Sébastien stops some ten metres from the fire engine where presently the firemen are aiming hoses at the flames.

Water is sprayed in wide angles over the burning area. The sizzling sound of water hitting fire comes his way, along with an intense smell of burning grass. He witnesses the firemen extinguish the fire until only a scorched piece of earth is visible. The flames have now disappeared but water is still sprayed over the black area. One of the firemen spots Sébastien and walks towards him. 'Bonjour. That was close, monsieur. Good that you called.'

Sébastien points towards the five figures in the distance, not far from the house. 'I have my men to thank for that,' he says.

'It's been so dry,' the fireman says as he wipes the sweat from his face, which leaves a black mark on his cheek. 'I'm sure this won't be the last fire we have to put out this season.'

Sébastien shakes his head. 'I think we'd better call the police for this one,' he says. 'I saw someone throw something and then the fire started.'

The fireman's face becomes grave, and he turns towards the scorched field. '*Mon Dieu*,' he sighs.

About an hour after the fire had taken place, the police arrived. After a close inspection, nothing could be revealed that indicated arson, but spontaneous combustion in the middle of a field didn't convince them either. They left the field after placing a red-and-white ribbon around the scorched circle. Sébastien wonders what that is going to solve. He now watches the police car turn and drive off along the unpaved road that runs parallel to one of the outdoor arenas, before he walks to the kitchen and enters the house. The rest of the men are having lunch, and sit around the rough wooden table on a bench they found in one of the sheds.

'Coffee, patron?' Nicolas asks him and he holds up

his Thermos.

Sébastien nods and sits down at the table. '*Merci.*' The man in the field and the flames that shot up keep mulling around his mind. 'Are you all sure none of you saw this guy go into the field?'

Some men shake their heads wearisomely; they had been asked the same question more than once this morning. 'He must've come from the forest,' Raymond says and breaks a piece off the baguette.

'The police will find who did it,' Nicolas states. He pours some white wine, that one of the men brought, into his cup. 'Nowadays they're very clever with their forensic investigating,' he says. He is the pensioner of the small group, but not in the least idle. The people in the village can always rely on him for help. Sébastien is certain Nicolas is right but is still concerned. 'Why would anyone purposely set fire to someone's property?' he asks.

None of the men are willing to discuss that question. 'Don't worry too much, patron,' Raymond says. 'We'll get this place back in working order. Do you have any horses yet, to stable here?'

It is a mystery to Sébastien where they obtained that knowledge and he answers: 'No, actually not. But, I'm sure my father can help me there.' He reaches out and takes a piece of the bread while Julien hands him a chunk of cheese. 'Better eat first, patron,' he says. 'Nothing goes on an empty stomach.' The men laugh and pour more wine into their cups. Nicolas slaps Sébastien on his shoulder. 'Come, eat!'

2

*T*he clock on the wood-panelled wall in the hall of the house at La Fontenelle ticks steadily as it shows the early hour. Sébastien looks at it while he comes down the stairs. He walks into the kitchen where he notices the remains of his father's breakfast still on the table. He had heard Pierre leave about ten minutes earlier. His parents' bedroom had remained quiet after that. He presumes Sylvia is still asleep. Sébastien pours himself some juice from a jug that is on the table. He takes the coffee pot with the remaining coffee and sits down. While he reaches for the bread in the basket, the phone on the counter starts ringing. Sébastien glances over his shoulder, expecting someone else to answer it, before rising from his chair to pick it up.

'Bonjour,' is all he says.

'*Grand-père?*'

Sébastien feels a quiver go through his body. '… Uh, no.' He braces himself. 'No. Cécile, it's me, your father. I'm afraid – '

'*Is Pierre in? Or Sylvia?*' his daughter demands. Sébastien understands the way she reacts towards him. It's her usual response on those rare occasions when she must deal with her father. 'No, Pierre left – '

'*Left? At this hour …?*'

'Yes, he must have some business. Cécile, I … I'm back at – '

'*Yes, I know. Grand-mère told me. Is she there?*'

'No. Well, I think she's still asleep.'

'*Can you tell her I called? I'll call back later.*'

'Cécile. I was just thinking, what if you … ' The

engaged tone rings in his ear. It had rung even before he had started his sentence. With a sigh, he puts the phone back on the receiver, conscious of the mistakes he has made but knowing that he doesn't love his daughter any less. The treatment she gives him, pains him. He wonders if she realises that, being a parent herself. He drags his feet back to the table when Sylvia comes in from the hall, still in her nightgown. 'Was that the phone?' she asks cheerfully.

'Yes,' Sébastien replies. 'Slept well?'

'*Oui.*' She notices Sébastien's serious expression.

'It was, uh, it was Cécile. She wants you to call her back,' he says, staring at his coffee cup. Sylvia glances at her stepson sympathetically.

'Sylvia,' Sébastien begins. 'Sylvia, I haven't been such a bad father, have I?'

Sylvia looks at him with an empathetic face. 'No. No, you just weren't there a lot.' She sits down at the table, too.

'I want to try, Sylvia. I *am* trying, but Cécile is so … so short with me always. I don't understand it.' He frowns. 'I know, I should have been there more often, but … Well.' He doesn't want to re-live the years after Natalie's death.

'Did Cécile say what she wanted?' Sylvia asks.

'No,' he says without looking up.

'I'd better give her a ring now,' she says as she gets up from her chair and picks up the phone. 'It might be urgent.'

While Sylvia hears her granddaughter on the other end of the telephone line, Sébastien abruptly stands up, strides to the door and goes outside.

'Good morning, sweetie,' Sylvia says and looks out the window to see Sébastien walking across the lawn.

'*Morning, Mamie ... Is my father gone?*'

' ... Yes,' is Sylvia's reluctant answer. 'Darling, can't you try and get along with him? He *is* your father.'

'*Please Mamie. Listen, I need to go abroad, big conference, and was wondering if you could take Thomas for a week or two. He won't be any –* '

'But of course, Cécile! We would love to have him!'

'*Fine. Thank you, Mamie. Got to run now, I've an early class. Bye!*'

'Bye darling.'

The following morning, Sébastien paces by the stables where stable hands and jockeys are busy saddling horses for their morning training. He hesitates when he's about to pass Jeune Homme's box but then goes in. He searches for the horse's gear and finds it nearby. After he has saddled the horse, he leads the animal out into the yard. 'Not too fast with him, Sébastien,' the trainer warns him.

'Don't worry,' Sébastien replies and swings his leg over the back of the horse. 'Just taking him for some exercise.' At a walking pace, he leads the horse out of the yard and towards the forest where he spurs him on. He is surprised by the way he eases back into his riding habit. The horse hasn't forgotten his professional life and at a steady gallop he rushes Sébastien through the wooded area, across the open grassland, and along the bridlepath through the pine trees until they reach the private beach. Jeune Homme trots along when he feels the loose sand underneath his hooves, and moves towards the water's edge. Sébastien squints his eyes now that the sun is shining sideways in his face. He thinks about his daughter Cécile who never liked horses, but she always loved the beach. He never really understood why she didn't feel much love for the animals, and at times it had annoyed him. It wasn't that any of the horses had ever frightened her. Maybe it had been their size. She was so small then, before her mother passed away. Without Sébastien urging him on, Jeune Homme picks up speed and continues to gallop along the edge of the water. With the horse's hooves hitting its surface, the seawater splashes up, leaving wet spots on his jeans. The briny smell of the water soothes his senses. It reminds him of how much he has missed that smell, too. At the far end of the beach, Sébastien pulls the reins; he hardly needs to guide Jeune Homme. At the low stone wall, which marks the end of the private beach, the horse turns around and gallops back the way they came. Sébastien notices a white blur to his left and he looks in the direction of the forest. He spots the white dog that has emerged from the trees, and is now running towards them. Sébastien feels his horse's nervousness and pulls the reins slightly. The white dog slows down and stops near them.

'Hello,' Sébastien says. 'Recovered, have you?' The dog lets out a short bark and wags his tail as his long fur waves in the sea breeze.

'Better go, Métèque, you're making my horse nervous.'

The dog looks up at him, and Sébastien catches his brown glance before Métèque walks on along the beach.

His thoughts go back to the days when he was a young lad, and playing here so often with his own dog. He turns around in the saddle to see Métèque running and splashing in the surf by himself. A smile slides across Sébastien's face. It seems as if time has not changed.

He sits back in the saddle and makes a clicking sound with his tongue. Jeune Homme gathers speed once more, and races along the tideline until they reach the forest where his horse, of his own accord, finds the way back to La Fontenelle. At the stables Sébastien releases the horse from his gear and leads him to a pasture nearby to allow him to remain outside. In the distance, he sees his father's horses race along the training track. At the insistence of the trainer the jockeys urge the horses to achieve the best results. Jeune Homme whinnies when he notices his congeners, then he bows his head and starts nibbling the grass.

Sébastien walks towards the house, and enters by the kitchen door where he finds Jeanette, the housekeeper, rolling dough. 'Bonjour, Sébastien,' she says.

'Morning Jeanette.' He looks at the empty basket on the table. 'Is there any bread left?'

'In the pantry,' she says as she keeps kneading.

Sébastien goes into the cool storage space and looks around for a nice loaf of bread. Right beside it he spots a few bottles of wine and takes one from the rack. When he has added a piece of cheese from the refrigerator to his items, he leaves the house and walks towards his car.

The dust settles around the tyres of Sébastien's car after he has parked in front of Café Villeneuve. When he is about to enter the café, he sees his father's car pulling up in front of his. At seventy-four Pierre is as agile as he ever was, and the years of riding have kept him as fit as a forty-year-old. He is quickly by his son's side. They both walk through the door and into the cool air of the establishment.

'Sébastien,' Pierre says, 'I just came from Jean-Luc's office – '

'Your solicitor?'

'Yes. There is nothing to worry about. That developer, Morgan, has nothing he can use against me. We only discussed the *possibility* for him to buy Les Jonquières.'

Pierre pulls up a chair, and they sit down at one of the tables. They're immediately spotted by the proprietor, and monsieur Beauchamp is already by their table. 'What shall it be, gentlemen?'

'Coffee, please,' is Sébastien's answer. 'Oh, and thank you for sending me those men.'

'Don't mention it,' Michèl replies. 'For you, anything,' he adds with a smile. 'And uh … I should thank *you*. Sorry about Métèque's harebrained antics. I hope there wasn't any damage to your car.'

Sébastien waves it aside. 'I'm just glad your dog is all right.'

'I'll have a sandwich with my coffee,' Pierre interrupts the amicable conversation.

'Coming up,' Michèl says and rushes off to get their order.

'Papa, how many people do you know who would want to stable their ageing racehorse?'

Pierre shrugs his shoulders. 'I'll have to look into that. Some just send their horses to the slaughterhouse, you know.'

Sébastien looks at him with disapproval in his eyes.

'But I'm sure there are empathetic horse owners too,' Pierre adds. 'Were you also thinking of training horses?'

'You know,' Sébastien says, 'I never was much of a horse trainer. Don't you agree?'

Pierre nods. 'You could hire someone.'

Sébastien shakes his head. 'I'd rather just ride them. I don't think I could take the pressure again of that, that constant effort to be the best with the best horse of the stables. I just want to live without all that stress for a while.'

Michèl Beauchamp comes to their table and places their order in front of them. '*Bon apétit,*' he says before walking over to another table to serve customers.

'What will you live on, then?' Pierre asks. 'Horse owners might not always be willing to pay for their horses' retirement, too. They'd rather just have them put down, to save money.'

'I'd hoped that horse owners wouldn't be so callous when it comes to the animals that have made them all that money over the years.'

Pierre laughs and pats Sébastien on his shoulder. 'Please, son! All these years in the big city and you still haven't learned?' He shakes his head. 'You always had a heart, for any animal, but don't think all horse owners have the same opinion as you.'

Sébastien is quite serious as he faces his father. 'Papa, more than twenty years ago Natalie seemed to think that people who owned horses were humane people. I want to believe she was right.'

Pierre places a hand on his son's arm. 'Natalie had the right notion,' he says. 'You go ahead. I'm sure, somehow, you will succeed.'

He starts eating his baguette, which is made with all sorts of cheeses and salad, when the door to the restaurant opens abruptly, and a balding man in his mid-fifties casts an interrogative eye around the room until he spots the two men at the table. He paces towards them and stops in front of them. Pierre looks up while Sébastien places his coffee cup back on the saucer.

'Maréchal!' the man demands. 'We had a deal! Where did you get the nerve to pull out of our deal?!'

He turns around and faces the other customers. 'Have you ever seen such an imposter!?' he calls out. 'A scheming dealer in lies!' His last words are accompanied by a harsh slap on the table. Sébastien's coffee splashes across its surface. The other customers in the café look towards the man with indignant expressions for his impudent disturbance of their peaceful assembly. Pierre's face turns pale and he stands up. 'Now, you stop it right there! We never had a deal! We only discussed some possibilities!'

Sébastien gets up as well and tries to calm his father. 'Papa … ' He catches his father's shoulder to move him away from the man who now grabs Pierre's arm.

Michèl Beauchamp, who has heard the loud voices from the kitchen, rushes towards the quarrelling men.

'Hey, hey,' he says in a calming tone as he pushes the angry man away from Pierre. 'Where are your manners, *hein*? Attacking an old man.'

Pierre is not amused by Michèl's last remark.

'He's right, Papa,' Sébastien intervenes. 'That man has no business attacking you like that.'

'Indeed he has not!' Pierre accedes, as he keeps an incensed glare on the man. 'Make yourself scarce! You, you … '

Michèl intervenes and pushes the intruding man towards the exit. 'No fighting and quarrelling in my establishment,' he says as he jockeys the man out of the door.

'You haven't heard the last of this!' the man yells before the door is shut in his face.

'I don't want that *émeutier* here in my place,' Michèl utters. 'Are you all right, monsieur Maréchal?'

Pierre nods affirmatively. 'Calling me an imposter,' he says disgruntled.

'Well, monsieur Maréchal,' Michèl expresses, 'we can't wait to see the back of him, I assure you. We all know what he intended to do once he got his hands on Les

Jonquières,' he says and walks back towards the kitchen. The rest of the customers mumble approbation now that peace has returned, and they too resume their previous activity. Sébastien entreats his father to sit down. 'Please, Papa, eat your lunch.'

With a certain reluctance Pierre sits down and takes a bite from his baguette before placing it back and shoving the plate aside. 'Have you heard any news about that fire at Les Jonquières?' Pierre asks in an attempt to resume their earlier conversation.

'*Non*,' Sébastien replies. 'The police haven't found any leads yet, but they seem certain someone set fire to it intentionally.'

Pierre remains quiet. The serious look on his face does not diminish. He reaches into his pocket and throws a few banknotes on the table. 'Let's go,' he says and stands up.

Michél is engaged with rearranging china behind the counter, and Sébastien says goodbye to him with a nod before he follows his father outside.

When Sébastien gets out of his car in the front yard at Les Jonquières, he is surprised to see a familiar car by the fence across the yard. The metallic green Renault is parked in the shade of a tree, and the owner of the car turns to face him.

'Angéline,' is his surprised reaction. He slowly walks towards her as she begins to approach him. 'Hello, Sébastien. How have you been?' She stops in front of him.

'Fine,' Sébastien replies. 'What brings you here?'

'Oh, hasn't Sylvia told you? I came to drop off Thomas.'

'Thomas?'

'Yes. Your grandson. You must know he stays with

Sylvia and Pierre on occasion.'

Sébastien can hardly remember the little boy; he has only seen him when he was a baby. 'And, what is this occasion?' he asks.

'Cécile had to go London for a conference. She flew from Paris, early this morning, so she thought it would be easier if *I* brought Thomas to stay with your parents.'

'Easier? Or is she just avoiding me?' Sébastien wonders.

A smile appears on Angéline's face as she moves her hand to shake a curly lock from her shoulders. 'Easier,' she then says.

Sébastien looks at her, then takes the food items from his car before proceeding to the house. 'Sorry, I can't offer you much,' he claims. 'We're still clearing up.'

'Oh, don't worry,' Angéline replies airily. 'Lovely place though. Imagine, spending all these years in Paris when all this while you had this lovely property here.'

'Look, I really don't have much time now,' Sébastien says. 'Why don't you come over when everything's finished?'

'Sébastien, I drove all the way from Paris. Don't brush me off like this.' Angéline is peeved by his manners.

'Sorry,' he says and walks into the kitchen. Angéline stops the door from closing and enters as well. 'There's no need to treat me this way, you know.'

Sébastien turns to face her. 'I said, sorry.' He places the bread, wine and cheese on the table. 'There's nothing for you here, Angéline, and I have work to do.'

Angéline gives him a stern look. 'You know what your problem is? You just can't take it that I *do* get along with your daughter. That's not my fault, Sébastien. That's your own doing!' She turns and walks out the door, slamming it behind her.

In anger, Sébastien slaps the bread off the table and sits down on the hard, wooden bench. He listens as Angéline's car turns and drives off the yard until the noise of the engine is out of earshot. Then, with a sigh, he gets up, reaches for the bread on the floor, and wipes some dust off it before placing it back on the table. He glances around the empty space and tries to remember what it was like some twenty-five years ago. His little girl played on the floor while his wife Natalie, almost always in riding pants, stood by the table preparing a meal.

'Patron! Ah, there you are,' he hears behind him. 'Patron, we're still waiting for that supply of wood.' Sébastien turns to see it's Nicolas entering the kitchen. 'It's all right,' Sébastien says. 'I only ordered it yesterday. Give it a few more days.' He walks out, followed by Nicolas. 'How are things going?' Sébastien enquires.

'Good. Julien's friend has come with his mower and is now at the back, mowing away. We're still in the stables. There's a lot of old stuff that can't be used anymore.'

Nicolas enters one of the stables, and Sébastien witnesses what he means. 'The stone structures are still fine,' Nicolas informs him. 'It's the wooden parts. My guess is, that the wood wasn't of the best quality. That, or it was never treated properly.'

Sébastien looks at him. 'You're probably right,' he says. When Les Jonquières was still under his father's control, worrying about the wood quality must have been the last thing on his mind. 'But, we can fix that,' he adds.

Nicolas walks outside and points to one of the sheds. 'That one,' he says, 'I think that one needs to go. It's a hazard, about to collapse.'

Sébastien remembers the shed, and how easily the door plank broke away on the day of the fire. 'You're right,' he says. 'Let's empty that one and then we can pull it down.'

After giving the property a closer inspection, it dawns on Sébastien that it is in a worse state than he initially thought, something he had not considered when he had planned to move back. He now understands why his father was in a rush to sell Les Jonquières. And he is grateful that his forefathers built the house with better materials. He would not want to lose the house.

'Will you be able to make these repairs, Nicolas?'

'*Bien sûr,*' Nicolas replies. 'But I do think that you should have a builder in.'

Sébastien concurs. 'Fine. Any suggestions?'

Nicolas nods and gives him a meaningful look, he then returns to the stable block to help the other men.

At the back of the stable block, Sébastien sees one of the men removing the tall grass. He obviously is not a novice. The entire field has nearly been cleared, leaving the scorched circle even more visible.

With little Thomas in her wake Sylvia strolls through the vegetable garden and gathers some vegetables. 'Come, darling. Let's give these to Jeanette, then she can cook us something nice.'

The boy follows Sylvia as they exit through the garden gate. He runs ahead of her towards the house when a car halts in the court. Thomas stops abruptly in his tracks and turns towards his great-grandmother. '*Une auto!*' he cries. Sylvia walks quickly to join him. 'That's Sébastien,' she says. 'Your grandpapa.' She takes the boy's hand. 'Let's meet him.'

'But Grandpapa is in his office!' Thomas says.

'No darling. That's your *arrière-grand-père.*'

'Arrière-grand-père,' the boy repeats after Sylvia.

'Hello, Sébastien,' Sylvia greets her stepson who is just getting out of his car. 'Busy day?'

Sébastien's eyes come to rest on the five-year-old boy by her side. 'Well, if you can call a renovation busy. Yes, it was a busy day.'

Sylvia gently pushes Thomas towards Sébastien. 'Come, say hello,' she instructs him.

Thomas stretches out his little hand. 'Hello.'

Sébastien smiles and looks at the boy. 'You've grown,' he says and pats the boy's light brown hair.

'Come,' Thomas says. He grabs Sébastien's hand, and they continue to walk towards the house. 'Jeanette is going to cook something nice for us.'

Sébastien turns his face towards Sylvia and smiles. 'Have you spoken to Angéline?' the latter asks. 'She hasn't returned.'

'Yes. Briefly,' Sébastien affirms, his smile evaporating.

'Jeanette!' Thomas cries as soon as they enter the kitchen. 'Grand-mère has v e g e tables for cooking!' He carefully pronounces the word that's not part of his usual vocabulary. Jeanette comes in from the hall and takes the basket from Sylvia.

'Thank you, Thomas,' Jeanette says to the boy. 'Were you good help?'

Thomas nods. Sylvia focuses on Sébastien. 'What happened? She was meant to stay for dinner.'

'She had to go,' is all Sébastien answers. He goes towards the fridge and takes a jug of ice-tea from it before placing it on the counter.

'Not on my workspace, Sébastien,' Jeanette informs him. 'Sorry,' Sébastien apologises. He places the jug on the table and takes a few glasses from the cupboard, aware of his stepmother's questioning eyes.

'Some ice-tea?' Sébastien offers and pours a few glasses.

'I think Thomas would rather have some lemonade,' Sylvia says. 'Sébastien, why do I have the impression – '

'Sylvia, she left,' Sébastien persists. 'Please, let's just leave it at that.' He sits down at the table, facing his grandson. He looks at the boy who in some ways reminds him of his daughter, even though he also carries unfamiliar features in his face. Sébastien has never met his daughter's boyfriend; he wouldn't be able to tell who Thomas resembles most.

'Do you ride horses?' Thomas asks him.

'You're not shy, are you,' Sébastien answers.

'*Quoi?*'

'Exactly. And yes, I do ride horses,' Sébastien replies. 'Do you?'

Thomas shakes his head. 'My maman doesn't like horses.'

'And you? Do you like horses?'

The boy shrugs his shoulders. 'Don't know. I never try.'

An amused glint appears in Sébastien's eyes. 'Maybe we can try, uh? Maybe you do like horses and you never even knew.'

'Please, Sébastien. Don't put any ideas into his head,' Sylvia intervenes. 'You know how Cécile feels about it.'

Sébastien shrugs off the remark. 'Why shouldn't he befriend the horses? He can hardly avoid them here, can he?'

The freshness of the following morning is a welcome change from the heat that has plagued the area for some time now. Sébastien enjoys the early hour and gallops with his horse along the forest track and onward, to the beach where he gives Jeune Homme reins. The horse takes full advantage of that freedom and shows what he is still capable of. They ride to the far end of the beach where, along a path, they could find their way to Les Jonquières but Sébastien decides against it. With a brief pull on the reins, he turns Jeune Homme around, and they gallop back towards La Fontenelle. Before leaving the sands Sébastien briefly casts a glance along the length of the beach and sees the white dog running along the water's edge. His paws splash in the shoal of the seawater that is rolling onto the beach. Sébastien smiles before continuing through the forest back to his parents' house.

When Sébastien rides into the yard at La Fontenelle, he finds another early riser. By the stables at the back of the house his grandson, Thomas, is looking around with an inquisitive expression on his face.

'Bonjour. Does Grand-mère know you're up this early?' Sébastien addresses the boy, who merely shrugs his small shoulders. 'She always sleeps late,' he says.

That is not entirely true, Sébastien knows, but he understands Thomas's inquisitiveness. The boy reminds him of himself in some ways. 'Well, since you're here, maybe we could have a look at the horses,' Sébastien suggests and dismounts.

'I already have,' Thomas says. He looks up at the large animal his grandfather just came down from.

'You have? Have you been inside the stables?'

'No. I can't reach.'

'Well, we'll have to do something about that, won't we.' Sébastien hands Thomas the reins. 'Here, you lead him back.'

The boy looks apprehensive and doesn't seem eager to lead such a large animal.

'Don't worry. He'll follow,' Sébastien reassures him.

He observes Thomas as a certain boldness appears in the boy's face while he takes the reins from him. Thomas's apprehension gives way to determination, and it is as if his grandson has always led horses back to their stables.

'Well done,' Sébastien says.

'When can I ride one?' Thomas asks.

'Are you serious? These animals are very high for a small boy like you.'

'I want to ride a horse,' Thomas says as Sébastien unsaddles Jeune Homme.

'We'll have to see about that, Thomas. It's not easy.'

'But I want to,' Thomas says.

'Maybe next time. When I go riding, you can sit in the saddle with me,' Sébastien promises.

Thomas's face lights up. 'Can I, Grandpapa?'

Sébastien smiles as he bends down and puts a hand on his grandson's shoulder. 'Yes, you can. You'll be all right when I'm with you.'

'I'm going to ride!' Thomas calls out. He runs and leaves the stable.

'Where are you going?' Sébastien wonders.

'Tell Grand-mère I'm going to ride a horse!'

Sébastien drops Jeune Homme's head gear and rushes after Thomas. 'Whoa,' he says and grabs the boy's arm. He stops Thomas and looks at him. 'Better not tell Grand-mère, Thomas. Better keep it a secret. OK? A secret between you and me.'

A conspiratorial look appears in Thomas's face and he nods. '*Un secret.*'

3

*W*here only a moment ago the stars could be seen as small specks with a thin slither of the moon among them, dark clouds are now rapidly obscuring the evening sky. The rumbling sound could be mistaken for the noise of speeding cars in the distance. Black clouds that loom in the west are coming intimidatingly closer. Trees bow down with the sudden force of the wind and the sky, that has been clear for some weeks, is now incapacitated and disappearing as blackness rolls across it. While the trees are being whipped in an easterly direction, drops of rain start falling to the ground. At first, the water droplets dry on the warm surfaces as soon as they find ground, but the rain rapidly increases, until curtains of water sweep across the area. The mass of dark clouds has completely taken over the once clear sky. Lightning whizzes through the darkness and briefly spreads an intense brightness that is reflected in the mirrors of rainwater. Almost simultaneously loud crashes of thunder follow.

At La Fontenelle Sébastien and Pierre have left the house, and are now running through the mercilessly beating rain towards the fields where most of the horses were left after their training. Stable lads run towards the rain swept fields, some carrying a horse halter in their hand.

'Over there!' Sébastien shouts above the loudness of the storm. He can barely distinguish where the animals are but is pointing in the direction where he spotted them when another bolt of lightning struck through the darkness. The horses are standing close together under the protection of some trees by the side of the field. Through the rain and the noise of the thunderstorm the men run towards them. The field has already become thoroughly wet and sodden, which makes it hard to move across. Pierre finds that his juniors are making their way across the drenched surface with less difficulty than he is.

'Get them away from the trees!' Sébastien yells and motions with his hand. 'Drive them towards the gate!' The men are completely saturated when they arrive at the refuge the horses have chosen. The animals are tense and move about nervously.

A few men stand in front of the horses, and wave their hands to make them move away from the fence. 'Careful!' Pierre yells. 'Here! Put that gear around Flaming Star's neck, he'll lead them.' Gérard proceeds, and approaches the black horse with the white marking between his eyes with soothing words and puts a halter around his head.

'Come, Star. Easy does it.'

The horse is ill at ease but allows Gérard to lead him onward. A short snort encourages the other horses to follow, and with a swift pace they leave the saturated field. Mud is splashing up from the hooves of the animals, and the men are not spared the sludge. Hands open stable doors, and one by one the horses find their shelter from the severe weather outside. 'Wipe them dry, men,' Pierre instructs. 'They should be all right now.'

Pierre presses his left arm as Sébastien stands beside him. 'Did you hurt yourself?' he asks. Pierre shakes his head. 'No, it's nothing. Let's get dried up.'

'You guys come to the house when you're done here,' Sébastien tells the men. 'Dry off and come have something to drink.'

Outside, the storm still rages as Pierre and Sébastien

rush to the house where Sébastien sees little Thomas in one of the windows. On entering the kitchen, they attempt to brush the rain off their attire but in vain as they're wet through.

'Please!' Sylvia calls out. 'Not here! Take yourselves to the bathroom and put some dry clothes on.'

Sébastien notices Pierre holding his left arm once more. 'You sure you didn't hurt yourself?'

'What a storm,' is his father's reaction. 'And so unexpected. Who'd have thought?'

Sébastien is concerned now that his father keeps evading his questions. 'Papa …' Pierre turns to face him. 'Son, not now.' Pierre continues into the hall.

'Plenty of people will be pleased with the rain, though,' Sébastien says as he follows Pierre. When he is certain that Sylvia won't be able to listen to their conversation, he addresses the issue again. 'Papa, what is wrong?' This time Thomas is the cause of the interruption.

'Grandpapa,' he says in a soft voice, approaching Sébastien. 'Grandpapa, when the rain is gone, can we ride a horse again?'

Pierre raises a questioning look in his son's direction.

'Maybe,' Sébastien says. 'Maybe tomorrow. Now, go to Grand-mére and uh … ' Sébastien looks at the boy as he indicates not to tell anything about their secret. Thomas understands and runs into the kitchen.

'Sébastien, do you think it's wise, teaching Thomas to ride? Cécile will be annoyed with you,' Pierre cautions.

'I'll worry about that when she finds out,' Sébastien replies and walks up to his room.

The following morning the evidence of the storm from the previous night shows that not only the land is well-watered, but that certain trees have been left uprooted in the forests around La Fontenelle. The skies have cleared overnight, and the sun eagerly tries to gain control again, and through her warmth, scattered clouds evaporate. In the course of the morning the noise of chain saws is heard through the trees. The local forestry department have started early and are continuing to assess and clear damaged trees. There, where the pastures slant downwards slightly, the rainwater found a way, and made constricted streams that have dried up in the sun, leaving desiccated forms snaking alongside the fields.

After inspecting the grounds around his parents' property, Sébastien now drives his car to Les Jonquières. Sitting in the backseat is his grandson Thomas, who opted for his grandpapa's company over that of great-grandmother Sylvia's. On entering the yard, Sébastien notices that most of the buildings here have been spared, and the house is left unscathed. Yet the barn that was declared a hazard by Nicolas is now partly hidden from view. A large tree that was near the structure rests on its collapsed roof.

'Grandpapa! Look!' Thomas exclaims.

'*Ça ne fait rien*, Thomas. We were going to pull that one down anyway.' They get out of the car, and while his grandson runs towards the damaged shed, Sébastien walks to the stables that all appear to have survived the storm. As he glances inside, he sees the large white dog snuggled up in some hay at the back of the stable block. 'Métèque?' he utters. 'Aren't you supposed to be at home?' The dog gets up and wags his tail. 'Don't tell me you've been here all night,' Sébastien says and strokes the dog's fur when behind him he hears his grandson.

'Grandpapa, Grandpapa!' his excited voice sounds. 'There's a big hole in the roof! That big!' He spreads his little arms out wide to convince his grandfather how big the hole is, until he notices the dog. The boy's reaction surprises Sébastien. Thomas, who usually displays a certain fearlessness, now has a frightened look on his face. 'Grandpapa. What animal is that?' He finds shelter by hiding behind his grandfather's legs.

'Thomas, that's a dog. You know what a dog is, don't you?'

'Yes, but this one is big.' He peeks around his grandfather in the direction of the dog.

'He's harmless, Thomas. Here, give me your hand and you can stroke him.' They move closer, and with care the boy touches the dog's fur. Métèque is undisturbed by the small boy's attention.

'See? He likes you, Thomas,' Sébastien tells his grandson. 'You know, when I was your age, I had a dog just like that.' Thomas strokes the dog once more, which Métèque acknowledges by pushing his head against the boy's hand, who smiles nervously.

'Come,' Sébastien says. 'It's about time Métèque goes home. It seems he's been here all night.' He leads the dog outside where he gently shoves him into the direction of the forest for the shortest way to the village. 'Go on, Métèque. Michèl will be wondering where you are.' Thomas rushes after his grandfather and waves his little hand. 'Bye, nice dog!'

A smile plays around Sébastien's lips as he sees Métèque run and disappear between the trees. 'Come, Thomas, let's have a look at that shed.' He takes the boy's hand, and they walk towards the structure that has seen better days. 'See, Grandpapa! See how big the hole is!'

From a safe distance, he estimates that it will need some strong hands and a machine to take down the shed and remove the tree. None of the men have arrived at this time but Sébastien imagines they may be helping others who have suffered damage. 'Let's go, Thomas,' Sébastien says and directs the boy back to the car.

'Are we going already?' Thomas asks.

'Yes.'

Thomas runs in front of his grandfather and grabs the door handle of the car. 'When are the horses coming?'

'Not until the stables are mended,' Sébastien says as he straps his grandson into the child car seat in the back.

'Are we going to live in your house then?'

Sébastien opens the door on the driver's side and sits behind the wheel. 'Would you like to?'

'If Maman wants,' Thomas says.

Sébastien starts the engine. He hesitates for a moment but then pulls out of the yard and onto the unpaved road that leads to the main road where Sébastien turns in the opposite direction of the village.

'Where are we going?' Thomas asks.

'I know of a man, he lives not far, who has a nice horse for sale.'

Thomas's face changes from excited to smiling, and he looks at his grandfather in a way as if they were sharing another secret.

'Actually,' Sébastien adds, 'it's a pony.'

'What's a pony?'

'A pony is a small horse,' his grandfather says, and steers the car through fields where young crops, to a large extent, have been flattened by the harsh rain. 'I thought, for a small boy like you, a pony might be better.'

Thomas has a twinkle in his eyes, and as Sébastien glances in his rear-view mirror he sees his grandson's face displaying the same boldness he has observed before. 'I only hope your mother won't object.'

'Maman doesn't like horses,' Thomas says. 'I'm not telling her.'

The sun has dried the land sufficiently, and the small outdoor ring at Jonquières is turned from a pool of mud back into the soft soil suitable for horses to trot around in. Thomas's face is red with excitement when his grandfather leads the pony, that is now his, into the ring. Thomas holds a black riding hat as he watches Sébastien fling the rein over the pony's head.

'Put that on your head,' he tells Thomas who quickly does what he is told, but when he struggles with the strap that should keep the protection on his head, Sébastien lends him a hand. 'Now, up you go,' Sébastien says, and lifts the boy into the saddle with one easy sweep. The boy's face gleams with pleasure. 'Go, go!' he cries out.

'Calm down, Thomas,' his grandfather says as he puts the boy's feet in the stirrups. 'Let's start from the beginning.'

He loosens the lunge line, and clicks his tongue for the horse to move outward along the fencing. 'Now, do as I told you. Move with the horse's rhythm,' Sébastien instructs. With a swiftness that comes with his age, Thomas moves too quickly up and down in the saddle. Sébastien shakes his head. 'No, no. Think of when you sat in the saddle with me. Go with the rhythm.'

The tip of Thomas's tongue appears between his small lips, and a severe, yet determined, look shows on his young face. He stops himself from going up and down in the saddle, which results in him being thrown about like a bag of potatoes. Sébastien hides a smile. 'No Thomas,' he says as he pulls the line and walks towards the boy and the pony. 'Thomas, remember when you were in the saddle with me?'

'You were holding me,' Thomas says.

'No, I wasn't holding you. I held the reins. You were

between my arms. Now try to remember how easy you sat in the saddle then.'

Sébastien walks back to the centre of the circle. 'Now, spur him on,' he tells Thomas. 'Just a gentle pressure on his flanks with your heels.' The boy follows his grandfather's instructions and slowly the horse starts moving again. Sébastien lets the line crack to speed the horse on, but when Thomas falls back by the sudden move forward, horror appears in Sébastien's face. Thomas remains oblivious of his grandfather's shocked reaction as he concentrates on holding the reins tightly. Sébastien utters a sigh of relieve when his grandson stays in the saddle. 'Well done, Thomas,' he says. 'Now. Move with the horse. Up on the right leg, down when his left leg is in front. Do you know left from right?'

With the understanding his age allows him, Thomas tries his utmost to stay in the saddle while following his grandfather's instructions. Sébastien leaves his grandson to find his ground; the boy is so young still. Maybe he shouldn't have encouraged him in the way he has. He remembers that he was four years older than Thomas is now when he first learned how to ride. Thomas hops up and down in the saddle, trying to ride to the best of his ability. His face is red with excitement and exertion. Sébastien pulls the lunge line, and the horse falls into a walk. 'That'll do for now,' he says. 'Or do you want to continue?'

Thomas turns his tired little face towards him.

'Alright then,' Sébastien says and lifts his grandson from the saddle. 'Did you enjoy that?' he asks as he undoes the strap on the riding hat.

'*Difficile*,' the boy replies.

Sébastien smiles. 'Well, I never said it was easy. Shall we tend to your pony now? That's also part of it, looking after your pony,' he says as they leave the ring with the horse following behind them.

'We will make a sign with your pony's name on it,' Sébastien says. 'To put on his stable door.' Thomas looks up at him with a happy face and seems to have completely forgotten that his first riding lesson was more difficult than he expected.

'Patron!' Nicolas's voice sounds and Sébastien sees him walk towards them. 'Patron, we can't continue with the supply of wood still not delivered.'

Sébastien frowns. 'Still not delivered? But they said … OK, I'll give them a call. Can you help Thomas look after his pony?' he asks and hands Nicolas the reins.

Sébastien feels in his pockets for his phone, then searches for the number of the *marchand de bois*, and dials it. 'Bonjour. Look, I ordered a whole supply of wood and planks a couple of days ago – '

'*Sorry, Sir, but do you have your order number?*' a kind woman's voice replies to his request.

'No, sorry. Can't you just find it by name? It's Maréchal. I came in personally to place the order.'

Sébastien listens to some shuffling, and the clicking of a computer keyboard on the other end of the connection.

'*Mais oui,*' he hears. '*Monsieur Maréchal?*'

'Yes.'

'*The order for four dozen beams and planks?*'

'Yes, that's it.'

'*Well, Sir, you cancelled that order.*'

'Cancelled? I never cancelled anything!'

'*I'm sorry, but someone cancelled the order three days ago.*'

'Look, that's a mistake. I never cancelled my order. I *need* that wood. Can you still deliver it?'

Sébastien hears the lady at the other end of the line sigh and mumble something under her breath. '*Monsieur Maréchal?*

'Yes.'

'*Monsieur Maréchal we can deliver it tomorrow afternoon, but it will be late in the afternoon.*'

'That's fine. Same supply. OK? Thank you.'

Sébastien turns his phone off, and a pensive expression arises in his face. He then walks into the stable where Nicolas is busy instructing Thomas how to take care of his pony after a training session.

'Nicolas! Nicolas, I don't know what happened but it appears that someone cancelled my order.'

Nicolas looks up while Thomas is absorbed in rubbing his pony's legs with a cloth; it is about as high as he can reach.

'I don't know how it happened, but I'm going to find out.' He proceeds towards the pony and takes Thomas by his hand. 'Thomas, I will have to take you back to Grand-mère.'

A mixture of bewilderment and disappointment appears in the young boy's face. '*Mais … mon poney.*'

'Nicolas will look after your pony,' his grandfather replies as he swiftly removes the boy from the stable. 'We'll come back tomorrow.'

With his expectations dashed, Thomas looks over his shoulder towards his pony as Sébastien decisively leads him to the car. 'I have some business,' his grandfather says. He puts Thomas in the passenger seat and straps him in with the seatbelt. The boy looks up at him with a disappointed expression in his eyes. 'Don't worry,' Sébastien says and he strokes his grandson's hair. 'Tomorrow you will have your *second* lesson.'

The *marchand de bois* is not far from the village. The grounds lie on the opposite side of Les Jonquières. Sébastien's gaze catches the piles of wood of various sizes as he drives towards the structure, that serves as an office, at the far end. He parks his car and then takes the few steps towards the small building. After a quick knock on the door, he enters and looks around to see a secretary behind her desk.

'Bonjour,' he greets her. 'I phoned earlier. Sébastien Maréchal.'

The young lady looks up at him. 'Ah, yes, you spoke to me. What can I do for you?'

Sébastien sighs before he proceeds, not certain if she will be cooperative. 'I would like to know if you could find out who made that call.'

'Monsieur?' the secretary questions.

'The person who cancelled my order,' Sébastien adds. 'You must have some record of it.'

The woman glares at him. 'I … I'm not sure if I can give you that information,' she says with uncertainty in her voice. 'We usually don't – '

'I need to know,' Sébastien presses and looks at her with piercing eyes.

'Well … ' taken aback, she gazes into Sébastien's golden-brown eyes. 'I uh, I can check my files … Phone numbers are usually stored.'

Her well-manicured hand moves the computer mouse, and she opens the files. 'What day did you say it was?'

'*You* said the order was cancelled three days ago,' Sébastien reminds her.

The young lady runs her eyes across the screen until she finds the correct day. 'I can't give you a list of all these numbers but I can print the one connected to you order,' she concludes. 'There we are.'

After a few more mouse-clicks, she prints a sheet of paper with Sébastien's order and an unfamiliar telephone number attached to it.

'*Merci bien,*' Sébastien says and he walks to the door, as the secretary watches him leave, 'bonjour, monsieur.'

Sébastien is about to open the door of his car when he looks at the information on the sheet of paper again. He searches for his phone but then decides against calling the number. He gets into his car and puts the sheet of paper in the dashboard compartment.

At Les Jonquières, the men are busy clearing the rubble of what once was the shed. The fallen tree has provided enough wood to help a few families get through a cold winter. Inside the house Sébastien decides to bring the work forward. The men have freed the inside from dirt and dust, and he now busies himself with painting the kitchen. He opens a bucket of paint and whisks the wooden spatula through the hue. Soon the light yellow that once enlivened these walls shows its true colour. He dips the brush in the paint and makes a few strokes on the wall. Stepping back, he inspects the result, giving it an approving look and then continues painting. While moving the brush along the wall, his memory drifts back to a day when he found Natalie occupying herself with the same task years ago. House painters were hired, but she insisted on lending a hand. She had chosen a light yellow for her kitchen walls and Sébastien now remembers her sweet smile. He had walked in, and she had turned her head towards him, momentarily interrupted by his entering.

'*Are we going to live in your house then?*' His grandson's question disturbs his thoughts. His daughter

Cécile was just a baby when this room was last decorated. Now Cécile's child asked him if they will live in this house.

'Yes, Thomas. If you want, we will all live here,' Sébastien says aloud to himself, and he dips the brush into the bucket containing the pastel yellow paint. He is suddenly gripped by the thought of how his wife Natalie would have felt about his neglect of their child over all these years. Only now does he realise she would have seriously disapproved. Sébastien stands breathless for a moment and the paintbrush stops. His shoulders drop, and paint drips from the brush onto the kitchen tiles. The anger he feels is directed at himself. Living the high life in Paris all these years while his own daughter was neglected by him. Sébastien shakes his head. He holds up the brush, the paint is now dripping down his fingers and he presses the paintbrush harshly against the wall. Then, slowly, he makes the required strokes that will cover the walls with a fresh coat. He climbs the ladder to be able to reach the higher sections near the ceiling. His arm moves along the wall, the brush leaving yet another clean beginning. The light yellow covers the grime that has accumulated through years of neglect, fresh yellow, sun yellow. Natalie's yellow. Ardently and persistently Sébastien moves the brush along the walls. Beads of perspiration appear on his brow, and sweat pearls on his chest, with sweat marks showing on the back of his shirt. He wipes his hand across his face and continues, dipping the brush in the bucket, moving the brush along the wall, one stroke after the next. The kitchen brightens with every stroke. When he has finally reached the beginning of his efforts, the door opens and Nicolas comes in. The smell of fresh paint penetrates his nostrils. He stops in his tracks when he sees Sébastien's achievement. 'P … patron,' he stammers. He looks around the bright walls, and he looks at the floor. 'Patron, one can tell you have not much experience with painting,' and he points to the marks on the ground. 'Better clean that before it dries.'

Sébastien now sees that the paint hasn't only cheered the walls but is splattered all over the floor.

'Next time better cover the floor with tarpaulin, patron. And maybe some head protection?'

'What do you mean?' Sébastien wonders.

'Your face.' Nicolas points to his own cheek. 'Yellow.'

Sébastien feels his face with his paint-covered hand, only to make it worse. Nicolas shakes his head and shoves Sébastien out the door. 'You'd better get cleaned up, I'll do that floor.'

Sébastien hesitates. 'Go on,' Nicolas insists.

Some of the men in the yard laugh when they see him pass. 'Why don't you tell me where I can find water and soap,' he says annoyed. One of the men points towards the stables. '*Voilá*, patron. In there.'

In the stables Sébastien finds a bucket of cold water and next to it, a bar of soap. He wets the soap and rubs it between his hands until the lather drips through his fingers, and his hands slowly return to their normal skin colour. Without a mirror, he can only guess where the paint has covered his face, and he roughly rubs his cheeks and forehead. His hair gets the treatment, too. With a cloth, that is normally used for horses, he dries up.

When he walks back to the house, Nicolas emerges from the kitchen, holding a mobile phone. 'Patron, your phone,' he says, 'it keeps ringing.' He hands Sébastien the device who sees that it is his parents' number on the display. 'Yes?'

'*Oh, Sébastien. It's Pierre.*' Sylvia's voice sounds

worried. '*The doctor has ordered an ambulance to take him to the hospital.*'

'Sylvia, what happened?'

'*It's his heart. I knew it. Please hurry home.*'

Sébastien looks at Nicolas. 'I have to go.' He strides over to his car. 'Those builders are due tomorrow!' he calls out to Nicolas before he gets into his car. 'Could you show them around?'

At La Fontenelle Sébastien finds his father sitting in his favourite chair with a pale, almost grey, complexion on his face. The doctor is by his side. 'Papa.' Sébastien rushes towards his father.

'Don't worry, son, I'm all right. They're making a fuss.'

'Pierre, we're not making a fuss,' the doctor says. 'This is serious.'

Sébastien looks at Sylvia who stands beside the chair, holding Pierre's hand. 'What happened?'

'Nothing happened,' Pierre answers.

'Pierre,' the doctor says.

'Papa, if nothing has happened, the doctor wouldn't be here, would he?' Sébastien tells his father. Pierre looks up at Sébastien, who notices his father's eyes appear dull. 'Papa, please, do what your doctor tells you.'

The situation reminds him of the time when he was still a boy and staying with his great-uncle, who also refused to take his doctor's advice. A few days later his great-uncle died in his arms.

Pierre remains silent while the doctor is on the phone, making arrangements for Pierre to stay in hospital and undergo treatment.

'Where's Thomas?' Sébastien asks Sylvia.

'He's with Jeanette,' Sylvia replies in a soft voice. 'I

don't want him to see all this.'

'The ambulance will be here any minute,' the doctor informs them as he puts his phone away. 'And you're going with them, Pierre. I insist. That heart of yours needs to be examined.'

'I don't seem to have much choice,' Pierre replies.

'No, Papa, you don't,' Sébastien says.

Pierre takes Sébastien's hand and squeezes it. 'Not to worry. I don't intend to go just yet.'

'Then do as your doctor says,' Sébastien insists.

Outside on the forecourt, the grinding of car wheels on the gravel can be heard, and the white from the ambulance is visible through the window. Sylvia quickly makes her way to the door to let the paramedics in as Pierre attempts to rise from his chair but his doctor places a hand on his shoulder. 'No rush, Pierre,' he says. 'Let them do their job first.'

While the paramedics take out the necessary equipment, Sylvia observes them helping her husband. When Pierre is comfortable in the gurney, they bring him to the ambulance. Sylvia and his doctor follow them close behind. Sébastien looks on as his father is pushed into the back of the ambulance. 'Look after yourself, Papa,' he says.

Soon after, he watches the vehicle drive off and then goes in search of his grandson. He finds him in the kitchen with housekeeper Jeanette. The boy is enjoying an early dinner of fries and lemonade. It seems he is unaware of what happened to his great-grandfather a little earlier. Thomas holds up some fries in an attempt to share his delicacy with his grandfather, who gladly accepts. '*Merci*. If you like we can go to Les Jonquières, and maybe have another riding lesson?'

Thomas's eyes glisten at the suggestion, and he

quickly proceeds to finish his food. Sébastien grabs one of the fresh rolls that are cooling on the counter and spreads some butter on it. He eats it while standing and waiting for his grandson to finish his fries, as Jeanette casts a questioning look at her tray of warm bread rolls.

4

Sébastien observes his brother François as he makes his usual entrance. Racing onto the court in his sports car, parking it where he stops, without being mindful that jockeys and horses might have to pass through there. François is generally engrossed in things other than the present, an absent-mindedness that seems to come with his profession. The tanned and wiry younger brother of Sébastien gets out of his car. His ordinarily dark hair is sun-bleached and shows a brownish hue.

'How are you,' Sébastien says as he embraces his brother.

'Fine. How's Papa?'

'Still in hospital. We can go there this afternoon if you want. He's going to be alright. He is still having some tests done.'

François looks about him and the place where he grew up. 'I was shocked when Maman called me. I didn't know he had problems with his heart.'

'He never let on. I didn't know either, until I came back and Sylvia told me,' Sébastien says while they walk into the kitchen.

'What do you mean, you came back. To stay?' François wants to know. He goes over to the fridge and grabs a cold drink.

'Yes, François. I have moved back to Les Jonquières. That is to say, we're refurbishing it. When the house is finished, I'll move back in.' He looks at his brother with a smile on his face, but François looks apprehensive. 'What brought this about?' François asks and he gulps the cool drink down. 'I thought Papa wanted to sell it?'

'How do you know? Papa never told us anything.'

'Not in so many words,' François states, 'but he has had the idea for some years now.'

'Some years?! How come I was never told? Why was I never made part of those plans? It was *my* home!'

'Never officially,' François says pragmatically. 'When you married and Maman inherited La Fontenelle, it automatically went to you. I was only twelve. No one ever consulted me, but I should have also had a say in it.'

Sébastien is stunned. He slowly sits down at the table. 'So … Wait a minute. Papa was more than happy when I came back and wanted to preserve Les Jonquières. He automatically assumed that everything would remain as it was.'

'Of course he would,' François says. 'But I'm also a son of our father. I should have a say in this, too!'

Sébastien looks at his brother disapprovingly. 'You could have let us know,' he replies in a critical tone. 'So, what do we do now? The property is still in Papa's name. When he gives it to *us*, what do you want to do? Live there as well?'

'Definitely not,' François replies. 'My family and I have a great house near the sea. But, you can buy me out,' he adds in a way that makes Sébastien wonder whether he ever knew his brother well.

'Buy you out?' Sébastien sounds resentful. 'We don't even know what the property is worth! You can't put a price on something like Les Jonquières.'

François remains stoic about the issue. 'That shouldn't be difficult. Finding that out, I mean.'

Sébastien gives his brother a stern look. 'We can't bother Papa with this problem now,' he then changes the subject. 'Let's give him time to recuperate first.' He gets up, frowning. He had never anticipated that his younger brother would have such a materialistic view about the situation. Without saying a word, he walks to the door and goes outside where he makes his way to the stables.

Not long after, his brother follows him there. 'Sébastien, be realistic. I'm not a horseman. I'm a marine biologist for Christ's sake! I love being near the sea! What would I want to do with a bunch of riding stables?'

'Nothing,' Sébastien merely says and proceeds to Jeune Homme's box but finds the horse has been put in the field. 'Want to come for a ride?' he asks of his brother, who rode a lot when he was growing up.

'Sure,' François agrees. They take a few horses from the pasture and saddle up.

Sébastien is the first to race his horse towards the forested area, soon followed by François who doesn't have a problem catching up, and together they race through the trees, across the heath, past the age-old Oak tree, and towards the beach. Sébastien, riding a younger animal, stays ahead of his brother, who enthusiastically urges his horse to win this race. Almost simultaneously they arrive at the sandy stretch where the sea has just withdrawn somewhat. François laughs loudly when he dismounts and drops onto the still damp sand. Sébastien follows his example and sits down too. Their eyes drift over the blue waters of the Mediterranean. In the distance, tourists are swimming in its waters and are sunbathing on the beaches, while a soft sea breeze wafts towards them, carrying a briny smell with it.

'Les Jonquières is near the sea too,' Sébastien observes.

François sighs. 'I know, but my daughter still goes to college in Marseille, my wife has a good job there, that she likes. As for me. Sébastien, we have our lives there.'

Sébastien moves his hand to push his horse's head away. The animal has started nibbling his shoulder. 'I hope you understand, but I never thought of putting a price on Les Jonquières.' He looks at his brother. 'I don't even know what amount Papa had in mind when he wanted to sell to that Morgan fellow.'

'What? Did he have an offer?' François sounds astounded. 'When was this?'

'Didn't you know? I thought you knew more about it than I did.'

François testily sticks a piece of driftwood deep into the sand. 'Papa never told me.'

'I was surprised too, when I came back,' Sébastien says. 'He was just about to call his solicitor. He said you were *definitely* not interested in Les Jonquières, and with me living in Paris – '

'It would've been better,' François mutters under his breath.

'What? What would've been better?'

'If he'd sold it,' François says, facing him. 'Then we wouldn't have this dilemma.'

'Please, François. Can you imagine what it would've done to the area? All those fancy apartments on Les Jonquières?' He shakes his head.

François remains indifferent. 'People have to live *some*where.'

'Holiday homes, François. Holiday homes that would've been empty for a large part of the year.'

There's a subtle change in François's conduct.

'Have you given it a thought? The amount, I mean,' Sébastien wonders, realising that his brother doesn't feel the same about the property as he does. 'I've made up my mind to stay.'

François averts his eyes and looks out across the sea

and along the beach. 'Let's go,' he then says, standing up. He grabs the halter of his horse before he reaches for the reins and mounts. Sébastien follows close behind and at a steady pace they make their way back to La Fontenelle.

The hospital grounds radiate a certain airiness as a soft, warm breeze wafts through the bushes, carrying the scent of flowers with it. Currently, Pierre is walking along a path, accompanied by his sons. His face shows a healthier complexion than it did a week earlier. They stroll along the flowerbeds through the pleasant garden. 'I'm glad you're receiving treatment now, Papa,' François says. 'You could've been dead!'

'Are you on medication now?' Sébastien asks.

Pierre looks from one to the other. 'Why is it that I have to end up in the hospital before my sons come to visit me?'

'Sorry, Papa.' François's face shows a degree of remorse. It's been over a year since he last visited with his job taking him abroad on several occasions.

'Cécile at least phones regularly,' Pierre says. 'There's nothing wrong with phoning, boys.'

Sébastien feels indebted to his father as well. 'Papa, we're both here now,' he repents. 'And … I hope you don't mind me bringing it up, but, François and I have discussed Les Jonquières, and we're wondering what would be the best thing to do.'

'What do you mean? Have you changed your mind?'

'No, Papa. But François feels that he should also have a say in the matter.' He glances at his brother, who takes a rather neutral stand, not desirous to trouble his father in his present state of health with the issue.

'Well boys, the matter is that I still own Les Jonquières and that you, Sébastien, promised to restore it to its former splendour and live there again.'

'But, Papa – ' François begins.

'There's no buts about it, François. I gave Les Jonquières to Sébastien, for reasons that he has an affinity for the property, and horses. Now, if you want, we can make that legal and I'll sign it over to Sébastien.' Pierre's decision appears to be final. 'I'm sorry, but that's how it is, François. Now if you think you have been left out, we've already willed La Fontenelle to you. So, all's fair and square.'

Pierre stops at a bench that is shaded by a tree and sits down. 'I hope we will not have any discord in our family now.'

Sébastien glances over at his brother with a contented look while François's face turns to surprise.

'Or did you think we'd forgotten about you?' Pierre asks of his son.

'Sorry, Papa,' François says.

'What would you have done with Jonquières, François,' Pierre wonders. 'Your affinity is more with seahorses.'

The sky is milky blue above them when Sébastien and François walk over to the car and get in. They both still feel somewhat sidelined after their father's account of his arrangements concerning the family property. Even though the outcome might be satisfactory, François still has misgivings. Sébastien presses the accelerator down, and they speed away from the parking area next to the hospital. 'I'm sure you want to see Maman,' he says.

His brother doesn't reply to that suggestion. 'How do you feel about all this, Sébastien? Papa taking matters in his own hands, making arrangements without consulting us.'

Sébastien shows more understanding of his father's decisions and shrugs his shoulders. 'Look, I have enough on my mind right now. If this is what Papa wants. And I'm sure he and Sylvia have both discussed it, I don't think it was just his decision. After all, La Fontenelle belongs to Maman.'

'That's not what I mean.' François sounds annoyed. 'The fact is that this is a family matter, and they never even asked us! What *we* want!'

Sébastien glances at his brother briefly. 'Would you have liked that? Would it have made any difference?'

François makes a deprecating sound and looks the other way while Sébastien takes in the scenery as the road veers slightly. 'Sorry, François, but I don't understand why it upsets you so. I was just as surprised when I returned home a few weeks ago, but I won't let Papa's decisions unnerve *me*.'

François doesn't respond to Sébastien's logic and looks out the car window. He spots a large white animal emerging from the forest, about to cross the road. 'Watch out,' he warns, but Sébastien has noticed the animal's actions. 'He's a bit off the beaten track,' he observes and slows down.

'Métèque!' Sébastien calls out through the open car window. The large white dog lifts his head in their direction and wags his tail at the recognition of the familiar voice.

'I'd better give him a ride,' Sébastien says and opens the back door of his car.

'Métèque, get in.' Without hesitation, the dog steps into the car and lies down in the backseat.

'Old friend of yours?' François asks with irony in his voice. 'You talk to him as if he's human.'

Sébastien pulls away from the side of the road. 'Don't

tell me you never talk to your dolphins.'

'Not habitually.'

'He belongs to Michèl. He owns the café in the village,' Sébastien clarifies. 'The dog is a wanderer but this time he has wandered too far from home.'

'He looks remarkably like the dog you used to have,' his brother says and casts a glance behind him and sees the dog lying comfortably, slobber dripping from his tongue. 'Judging from pictures you had of him.'

'He might be a descendant of Belle. Given that she once had a litter.'

'You think so?' François wonders.

'He could very well be. I was shocked when I first saw him. Shocked because he reminded me so much of good old Belle.'

They turn a corner and see the village ahead of them. Not long after Sébastien pulls up in front of Café Villeneuve. Métèque jumps out of the car as soon as Sébastien has opened the backdoor. The two men follow the animal as he walks into the café. Inside, Michèl is busy tending to customers when he notices his dog. 'Where have you been? You old vagabond.' The dog wags his tail and walks through to the kitchen. Sébastien and François take a seat at one of the tables, and it doesn't take Michèl long to wait on them.

'He had wandered off, out of the area,' Sébastien tells Michèl. 'He was halfway to Nice this time.'

Michèl shakes his head. 'I hope he's not going to make a habit of it or I'll have to tie him up. So, how's monsieur Maréchal?'

'Doing better,' François replies.

'François! How have you been?'

'Fine,' is the curt answer. 'Can we have some wine and bread?'

'I'll have an ice coffee, please, Michèl,' Sébastien says.

'Coming right up.' Michèl goes to the kitchen to get their order.

Sébastien looks at his brother who is sitting opposite him at the table, and who now faces him. 'Sébastien, it's not just Papa making decisions without making us part of them, but … Well, we, my wife and I, had hoped that one day Les Jonquières would be sold, the money divided between us and – '

'Sold!? François, Les Jonquières has been in the family for generations!' He gives his brother a thorough look. 'Why? Do you need the money? I can hardly believe that.'

'It might've been in the family for generations, but that didn't stop Papa from accepting an offer on the property without hesitation,' François reasons.

'He didn't really want to sell,' Sébastien argues. 'He was glad I showed up when I did.'

François looks at him with piercing eyes. 'Yes, he might've been, but why didn't he consult us then? What if you had decided to stay in Paris and had come for a visit to find that Les Jonquières didn't belong to the family any more. How would you have reacted then?'

Sébastien sighs. 'That scenario has crossed my mind,' he softly says. 'But then I remembered that Papa has always been like that. Making decisions on his own, rationalising they were always for the best.'

'And what was his rational idea behind this latest plan?'

'Age. François, Papa will be seventy-five this year. He's retiring. And admit it, the both of us haven't shown much … enthusiasm, either in the business or even in just coming home to visit.'

Michèl approaches their table with a tray. '*Messieurs*,' he says and places coffee, wine, cheese and a basket containing croissants and a baguette in front of them. '*Bon apétite.*'

'Thank you, Michèl,' Sébastien says.

'We've always been busy with our own lives, and jobs,' François says and pours himself a glass of wine. 'Papa and Maman understand these things, and you, you never wanted to come back.'

Sébastien feasts on the croissants and takes a sip of coffee before he asks his brother: 'What did you mean by *the money divided between us?*'

François breaks out in a cough when a gulp of wine gets stuck in his throat.

'Here, have a piece of dry bread.' Sébastien hands him some of the French loaf. As he watches his brother chew the bread, he waits for an answer.

'Well, that would have been the course of action, wouldn't it?' François replies.

'And that you and your wife *hoped* that Les Jonquières would be sold?' Sébastien looks at his brother with an accusing yet questioning glare in his eyes.

'Alright. Alright, there was a time, a few years ago, when we had some money problems … And then Louise hinted that, that there was actually quite a bit of money to be made if Les Jonquières … that was just sitting there idle,' François's voice lowers to almost a whisper, 'that it would be sold.'

Sébastien shakes his head. 'So, your wife put the idea in your head.'

François gives him an indifferent look. 'At the time, it was an excellent idea. And it still is,' he adds.

'You can't mean that.' Sébastien is taken aback by his brother's indifference. François shrugs his shoulders and looks at him. 'Does it matter now? Papa has settled everything. All's done and dusted.'

Sébastien gets up from his chair and takes some money from his pocket while he walks towards the bar where Michèl is cleaning glasses. '*Merci bien*, Michèl,' Sébastien says and hands him the money.

'You're welcome, Sébastien. Always happy to serve you,' but with a disparaging look he glances over to their table, where François is just standing up.

When the two brothers enter the kitchen at La Fontenelle, Sylvia turns towards them and her face lights up. 'François! Pierre told me you'd come home.' She takes his face in her hands and kisses him on both cheeks. 'You're home half a day and you didn't even come in to say hello.'

'You were out shopping with Thomas, Sylvia,' Sébastien says. 'Where is the little one, by the way?'

'As soon as we came back, he rushed out to the stables,' she replies. 'Have you two had your lunch?'

François holds his mother by her shoulders. 'Don't worry about us, Maman. We had something to eat at the café.'

Sébastien observes François, who feels his brother's glare. François isn't eager to address the issue they've been discussing earlier but turns to face him. At the same time directing the matter to his mother. 'Maman, Sébastien and I have been wondering why we were never consulted about the sale of Les Jonquières.'

Sylvia's face changes to surprise as she looks at Sébastien and François in turn.

'It's mainly François, Sylvia,' Sébastien says. 'He is upset because we were not asked when Papa wanted to sell family property.'

'But, nothing will be sold,' their mother says.

'No, because Sébastien came back!' François retorts, pointing at his brother. 'Where does that leave me?'

'François … ' Sylvia stammers. She directs her eyes towards Sébastien for support but he looks at his brother in earnest. 'Now, I wish you would tell us François, why you are so adamant about this. You heard Papa, I get Les Jonquières, you will inherit La Fontenelle. Eventually.'

For a brief moment François seems indecisive but then he turns abruptly, and walks out the door that slams shut in its post.

'What's with him?' is Sylvia's bewildering reaction.

Sébastien raises his eyebrows. 'I haven't a clue. If anything, I'd say he has money problems.'

'I find that hard to believe,' his mother says. 'He earns decent money. And he lectures at the university – '

'Yes. But he married Louise.' He looks at Sylvia with a knowing glance in his eyes. His mother returns the look. 'But, isn't there a way we can help François?' she broaches the subject. 'He's not himself.'

'I'm not going to give him any money,' Sébastien says, 'for his wife to spend it? No, this is between him and Louise.'

'You could be right,' Sylvia says before Sébastien, too, walks towards the door and goes outside. In the court, he looks around for his brother and notices that his car is still parked where he had left it before he walks towards the stables.

'Grandpapa!' he hears the clear voice of his grandson from one of the boxes. 'Grandpapa, I'm helping with the horses!' The boy's happy face appears in front of him.

'Excellent, Thomas,' Sébastien says. 'May I help too?'

The boy grabs his hand and pulls him inside one of

the boxes. 'This one needs food,' Thomas instructs as if he were a real pro. Sébastien smiles 'coming up, patron,' and makes his way to the bags with horse feed. When he reaches the far end of the stable block, where the feed is kept, he sees his brother sitting in a dark corner on a bale of straw, leaning backwards against the stone wall.

'François?' He walks towards his brother who turns his face away from him. 'François. Let's talk about this. No use sitting here repining.'

When his brother doesn't respond to his plea, Sébastien continues: 'Is it Louise?'

There's a slight change in François's demeanour. 'You guessed it,' he says. He briefly glances up at Sébastien. 'But that's not your problem,' he decides.

'Fine. Do you want to give us a hand with the horses?' Sébastien asks.

When François doesn't reply, he walks away but soon he hears his brother following him. 'I think I'll just take a horse out for a ride,' François says. He grabs one of the saddles and gear, and before long Sébastien sees him galloping along the track and going into the forest.

Daylight rapidly makes way for the darkness that now wraps the house in obscurity, save for the garden lamps and the light that falls through the kitchen windows. Inside the house, they hear the sound of a horse in the yard, and Sylvia looks up from the dinner table with a relieved face. 'Jeanette,' she says, 'that must be François. Can you please take his plate from the oven?'

They listen attentively to the sound of hooves on the gravel. The tread is slow, and the horse is almost dragging his way to the stables. Sébastien gets up to have a look outside and sees a lone horse passing by a garden lamp. He goes outside where one of the stable lads has also noticed the horse and takes him by his halter. Sébastien looks around for its rider, but can't distinguish much in the dark forests surrounding La Fontenelle.

'Sébastien,' the stable hand addresses him. 'Who was riding Sultan this afternoon?'

'My brother,' is the worried reply. 'Albert, can you get a few men together? I think we need to search the woods for François.' He then turns and hastens back to the house.

Sylvia stands in the doorway. Thomas is half hidden in her skirt, yet curious to know what's happening. 'The horse came back without its rider,' Sébastien says. 'We will need some lights.'

'François?'

Sébastien doesn't respond, not willing to worry his mother unnecessarily. He looks around in the pantry and comes out with two torches. He runs back to the stables and hands one to Albert. 'Saddle some horses,' he says. 'I've no idea where he could be, but he might be lying somewhere wounded.'

'Very well,' Albert responds and the men get busy while Sébastien saddles his own horse. He soon spurs the animal to a gallop, racing towards the forest. The light of the torch dances like a firefly through the dark pines. The flickering light is the only indication that someone is moving between the trees. Every so often he slows down and calls out his brother's name. To no avail. There is no reply. Sébastien feels fortunate that he knows the woods well, and he makes his way through its blackness towards the beach. It's a dark evening, and only the glow of the disappearing daylight behind the surrounding hills casts some lustre on the beach and rolling surf. Sébastien restrains his horse and proceeds at a walking pace, scrutinizing the sandy beach for a human figure. He shines his torchlight ahead, hoping it will draw his brother's attention. 'François!' his voice thunders over the quiet, rippling surf. His horse is startled by his voice and throws his head back. Sébastien pets his neck to calm him.

'François!' he calls out once more over the beach, which otherwise seems empty. At a slow pace, they continue until Sébastien has reached the low wall near the path leading towards Les Jonquières. The bushes bordering the beach don't reveal much, and the forest sweeping up behind them is a deep dark purple. With the flashlight tucked underneath his arm, Sébastien follows the path that, as a child, he used so often. It's still trodden and flattened by animals that walk along it. The beam of light from the torch casts phantasmal shadows through the black tree trunks, only making the surroundings appear more secretive. Sébastien stops his horse whenever he hears the slightest sound. 'François!' his voice echoes through the darkness. He listens, but there are only the birds of the evening screeching and a dried branch falling to the forest floor. A worried sigh escapes from his lips as they slowly move on. The path leads to the grassland that cuts through the forest, dividing the two properties. Sébastien now sees lights moving through the trees on the far end of the green. He gives his horse spurs and races towards the other side.

'Albert! Albert! Have you found anything!?' he calls out even before he has reached the wooded area. A few light beams shine towards him as he treads into the first row of trees, his horse becoming skittish because of the flickering lights. Albert is the one who nears him first. 'Sorry, Sébastien. Nothing.'

'I've checked the whole beach, nothing there either,' Sébastien replies. 'Maybe we have to spread out more.'

'I'll send one of the men to the village, for more

help,' Albert says. Sébastien nods. 'I'll have another look on the Jonquières side. Best follow me and we'll scour that area.'

With a pull on the reins, Sébastien turns his horse around. A hurried command from Albert sends one of the men in the opposite direction while the rest follow Sébastien. They gallop across the grassland to the other side, spreading out as they go and entering the natural environment of the woods where no paths are laid down. Step by step the horses find their way as they pass through the trees, and the men shine their torchlights into every possible corner where a person could be lying on the forest floor. They meticulously comb the area until they've reached the house and its adjacent stable blocks at Les Jonquières. Some of the men feel despondent because of their fruitless search, but Sébastien doesn't want to give in to the feeling that searching for François is hopeless on this moonless night with the forest so dark around them.

'The others might have more luck,' Albert tells him, in an attempt to boost Sébastien's spirits, and to indicate the situation isn't entirely hopeless. 'I'm sure Jérome has continued the search with the villagers' help.'

Albert's remark sends Sébastien racing towards the forest, where he takes a path that leads to the village. He can hear the rest of the men galloping behind him as they make their way to the wooded area that surrounds the small town. Not for long, they see lights through the trees and people calling François Maréchal's name. Most of them are on foot, others drive their cars along the road that borders the pine forest, with their headlights illuminating the surrounding area.

Sébastien leads the men from La Fontenelle until they all encounter each other in the woods, somewhere halfway between Les Jonquières and the village. Albert doesn't think further search will be productive and looks at Sébastien. 'I'm afraid we have to call it off. We've been everywhere. If he is somewhere in the woods, he would have heard us.'

'*Non!*' is Sébastien's dogged reply. 'He could be lying somewhere, unconscious. In need of medical help!'

'Patron.' This time it is Nicolas trying to convince him to abort the search. 'The people from the village have looked everywhere, too.' The villagers that have gathered look disappointed, but realise that a further search under these circumstances is futile.

'We have to keep trying!' Sébastien calls out, annoyed by everyone else's lack of perseverance. He spots Michèl Beauchamp standing among the villagers with his wife, but the man shakes his head. Sébastien's eyes glide around the group of people, most of them turning to go back to their homes. 'At first light, we'll be back,' Michèl lets him know before he, too, turns around to go home. Everyone from the village is slowly walking away. The men from La Fontenelle direct their horses back home as well, leaving Sébastien standing by himself. After a minute or so he too spurs his horse into a trot. He understands everyone's justification that this search in the dark seems hopeless, but he decides not to follow the others. He makes his way towards a corner of Les Jonquières that has not been searched. He urges his horse on, and they disappear in the darkness of the forest. Only the fading beam from his torch shines some light into the dark night. When he sees the contours of the house and adjoining buildings shimmering in the darkness to his far left, he notices something white drifting through the trees ahead of him. Sébastien shines his torch in that direction and his spirits are lifted when he sees it's the white dog. 'Métèque!' The dog does not acknowledge his call and walks on. Sébastien calls out once more, but the dog keeps walking, picking up pace. 'Métèque!' Sébastien spurs his horse into a gallop, and he starts to doubt if this is the dog he has befriended when the animal doesn't show signs of recognising his voice.

Suddenly a loud barking pierces the darkness and Sébastien hurries onward. Then he sees the white dog, sitting between some trees and barking loudly.

Sébastien jumps from his saddle and walks towards him. 'Calm, Métèque, quiet. You're scaring my horse.' The dog lets out another short bark and looks up at him. It is now that Sébastien sees someone lying on the ground. He shines his torchlight at the figure and straight in the face of his brother. He kneels down next to François and feels his arm that is cold. 'François!' He now notices that the dirt on his brother's face is in fact dried blood. 'François!' For a moment he is gripped by fear, and he feels his brother's chest for a heartbeat. Relieved, he starts to dig through his pockets for his phone. Within a few minutes he has given the emergency services the details of his brother's condition, and their whereabouts.

'François,' he says but his brother shows no signs of consciousness. Sébastien takes off the thin jacket he is wearing and drapes it over his brother. 'Métèque,' he says and the dog comes to his side. 'You deserve a medal,' Sébastien says as he pets the dog. 'Well done!' He then directs the dog to lie down by his brother's side to keep him warm. 'Métèque, you stay here,' he instructs the dog. He ties his horse to a tree and walks away, looking behind him to make sure that the dog stays where he is, watching over François. '*Restez lá*, Métèque. I won't be long!' Relying on his instincts, Sébastien runs through the trees towards a point where the road is closest to where he found his brother. He stops by the side of the road and waits. He starts pacing as the minutes pass, but only the quiet darkness surrounds him. Nervously, Sébastien continues pacing up and down until, at long last, he hears the siren of the ambulance. Its headlights shine like beacons on the dark road. Sébastien signals with his torch where they should stop. 'In here,' he motions when they slow down.

'Are you the one who phoned us?' one of the men yells through his open car window.

'Yes! Hurry, he's not responding!'

The paramedics remove the stretcher from the ambulance and follow Sébastien into the woods. When they reach the spot where François is still lying motionless, the paramedics are surprised to see a large dog serving as a shield and a horse keeping watch. They quickly go to work, and François is strapped to the stretcher, covered with a thermal blanket. 'Can you tell me what's wrong with him?' Sébastien asks. 'Will he be all right?'

'He had a blow to the head, doctors at the hospital will be able to tell us more,' and they continue walking back through the forest, as Sébastien lights the way with his torch; its light is now fading fast. 'What hospital are you taking him to?' he asks when they reach the road.

'Parc Impérial,' one of the paramedics replies.

'I'll get my car and then I'll come straight over to the hospital.' Sébastien has one last look at his brother before they slide him into the ambulance. He then returns and walks back through the forest to where he left the animals. Métèque has remained on his spot. Sébastien pets the dog's head 'come', and pulls himself into the saddle. With a short pull of the reins he starts leading the animals back to La Fontenelle.

When he enters its court, he calls out for Albert, but

it's Sylvia who comes running out of the house, with anguish in her face. 'Sébastien! Sébastien, tell me he has been found. Tell me my son is all right!'

Sébastien slides out of the saddle and his subtle smile says enough. 'But he's not all right. I'm going to the hospital now. Albert!'

Together with one of the men, the stable hand comes running. 'Has he been found?'

'He has. And this dog here deserves a medal.' Sébastien puts his hand on Métèque's head. 'He led me to my brother.' Sylvia is amazed and showers the dog with praises. Albert takes the horse back to the stables as Sébastien and Sylvia get into the car and drive off in the direction of Nice.

Two days after the operation François opens his eyes. Dazed and disoriented he looks around the room until his eyes rest on his father's face and an unknown figure beside him. His eyes close again, and Sylvia gently squeezes his hand. 'François,' she says softly. His eyes slowly open and he sees his mother sitting by his bed; a weak smile plays around her mouth.

'How do you feel, monsieur Maréchal?' the doctor asks. François looks at him but he doesn't answer. 'I'll come back later,' the man tells Pierre. 'He's still confused.'

As the doctor leaves the room, Pierre takes a seat on the other side of the bed. 'François. François, do you remember what happened? Sébastien found you in the woods at Jonquières.'

François looks at his father with dull eyes. 'Did you fall off your horse?' Pierre asks. 'Try to remember, François,' he presses.

'Pierre,' Sylvia warns.

François looks at her. 'Maman,' he utters, barely audible. For a moment, he closes his eyes. 'I ... I don't remember. How did I get here?'

'You're in the hospital, darling,' his mother says gently. 'You had an accident when you were out riding.'

François stares ahead. 'No, I don't ... ' he utters. 'I can't remember.'

'Don't worry, François,' Sylvia says. 'It'll come to you. Just rest, that's all you need, is to rest.' She looks over to Pierre. 'I'll stay here,' she decides. 'You tell Sébastien.'

Pierre carefully lays a hand on his son's shoulder. 'Your mother is right. Just rest. I'll see you tomorrow.' He gets up and quietly leaves the room. In the corridor he finds Sébastien talking to François's physician. 'Thank you, monsieur docteur,' Sébastien says as the doctor goes to attend to the rest of his daily tasks.

'Has Louise come yet?' Pierre wonders. 'What kind of wife is she anyway?' he adds with resentment.

'She should be on her way now,' Sébastien says.

They leave François's room behind them and walk out of the corridor. Since his brother's accident, Sébastien has spent more time at the hospital than at home, but is relieved that François has now regained consciousness. Pierre leaves the hospital to see to business at home while Sébastien takes in the fresh air wafting through trees outside, awaiting his sister-in-law. After half an hour, he sees her driving in her Porsche, looking for a parking space at the hospital. She gets out, and Sébastien walks towards her. 'Why did it take you so long to visit your husband?'

Louise looks at him, indignantly. 'Well, hello to you too, Sébastien,' passing him and walking towards the entrance. She is dressed in the latest Paris fashion, and her face and dark hair look impeccable. No doubt she came straight from the beautician and the *coiffeur*. 'Louise!'

She stops and turns around. Her green eyes show a certain disdain when she looks at him. 'There's no need to pretend any longer, Sébastien. I don't know what François has been telling you, but our marriage is as good as over.'

'Well, I got the impression that François thinks otherwise.'

'He just has to face up to reality,' Louise says plainly and begins to walk to the hospital.

'Louise! Now is not the time.' He grabs her arm. 'If you only drove all this way to upset him, you'd better turn back.'

She removes his hand from her arm. 'Don't worry. I'll behave. Like any concerned wife,' she says apathetically.

Sébastien watches her as she walks into the hospital and requesting something at the information desk. Instead of waiting for Louise to leave, he decides to go to Les Jonquières and check on proceedings there.

After a drive through sun-drenched scenery, he enters the yard and is pleased to see that work has continued, despite his absence. As he gets out of his car, he looks around for Nicolas. He sees him by one of the stables with the other men, who are carrying a few planks inside. Sébastien walks up to them and follows them inside to admire their efforts. 'Great job, guys,' Sébastien says. His hand glides over the newly constructed horseboxes that are clearly built with craftsmanship.

'How's François?' Nicolas asks as the other men turn inquisitive faces in Sébastien's direction as well. 'Doing better, he woke this morning,' Sébastien replies. He continues to the house and enters through the kitchen door. The brightness of the room is an invitation for family to gather there again. For now, the long wooden table on one side, surrounded by benches and the new, fitted kitchen, serves as a welcome space for the men to have their breaks in.

When Sébastien visits his brother in hospital on the following day, he finds him sitting up in his bed, and colour has returned to his face. The brothers embrace, and Sébastien grabs a chair and places it beside the bed. 'How've you been feeling?'

'Better.'

Sébastien looks at his brother and decides to bring up the subject of François's health. 'I was talking to your doctor the other day. One thing he mentioned was that, that you had a high level of antidepressants in your blood.'

François averts his eyes, 'I've been on them for some time,' he says before he becomes quiet.

'You can tell me, François.'

All of a sudden, tears appear in François's eyes. 'I'm such a failure!' he calls out in anger.

Sébastien puts his hand on his brother's arm. 'You're not. Don't even think it.'

'But I am!' He sounds annoyed, grabs a corner of his sheet and wipes his face, for a moment forgetting the bandage that is around his head. 'Damn! Everything I've done has turned into a fiasco. I can't even keep my marriage together.'

'Don't – ' Sébastien begins.

'I've tried and tried.' He faces his brother. 'I've done everything to keep her happy.'

'Well, she may not be worth your efforts.'

The anger in François's eyes intensifies, but then fades. 'You know what is worst? Realising that someone you love and thought you would share the rest of your life with only wanted you for the money you were earning, the prestige that came with it … And now, she has brought me to the brink of bankruptcy,' he softly adds.

In a way, Sébastien can identify with his brother, to lose someone you love. With a sigh, François falls back into his pillow and for a moment he closes his eyes. 'I don't really know what brought me to Jonquières that evening,' he then says. 'I raced and raced that horse, poor animal must've been at the end of his tether. And suddenly, something hit my face … ' He looks at Sébastien. 'That's all I remember.'

'Don't worry about it any longer, and the horse is fine. Even though he came back without his rider.'

François smiles faintly. 'I'm sorry.'

'Don't be. Just get well again.' He stands up to leave. 'Sylvia will come by later.'

He is about to open the door when François calls his name. 'Sébastien. I think Papa acted wisely. About the properties, I mean.'

5

*C*louds hover dull above the landscape as Sébastien walks onto the front yard at Les Jonquières. He notices the men, who have gathered under a tree in the yard, enjoying coffee and wine. 'Afternoon,' he greets them. A glance towards the field tells him that the shed is gone, and alongside the empty spot, a pile of logs is visible. He sits down on the bench beside the men.

'We're having some problems in the stables,' Raymond tells him. 'The wall at the back is a bit eroded. It needs to be dealt with first.'

'Is it serious?' Sébastien wonders. 'Not the whole block I hope.'

Nicolas stands up. 'Come, I'll show you.' Sébastien follows him as they stroll to the stable block. While they go around it to the back, they are enveloped by the shade of the canopy overhead. 'A damp spot, this corner,' Nicolas says. 'The sun hardly shines here, under the trees.' He takes out a pocket knife and scrapes it along the eroded wall; cement easily comes away. Nicolas takes a few steps back and points at the corner. 'I'd say, up to here. It's only this corner that has the problem.'

'I see,' Sébastien says. 'As I remember, this part was added once. They used bricks.'

Nicolas points at a supporting beam. 'We could break those bricks away from the beams. But we would need building blocks to replace them.'

Sébastien nods. 'I'll talk to the builder. Thanks.' They walk back to the others as the first drops of rain start to fall. The men walk to the kitchen door and enter the house, where Nicolas and Sébastien follow them. Not long after Sébastien decides to explore the house and check the rooms he hasn't been into since his return. Up until now he has been apprehensive, and found the prospect of going over every nook and cranny in the house rather daunting. He walks to the back of the house where the living-room is situated. They hardly ever sat there as the kitchen was always the main hub of the house. It's bare of furniture and the windows look dusty and dull. The door at the other end brings him into the broad stone-floored hall. His daughter loved to race her tricycle here, and they could hear her screeching with pleasure as they sat in the kitchen. The hall has another flight of stairs going to the first floor that Sébastien now takes. Some staff members used to have their bedrooms up there. Sébastien opens the doors to each room that open out onto the landing. They're mostly all the same size, spacious and some with, now grubby looking, basins. He bangs the side of his fist against one of the stone walls. Dust is dispersed into the air, but the wall doesn't give way a millimetre. Satisfied, he moves on, and walks around the corner where the private quarters are situated with his and Natalie's bedroom. There's another staircase, one that leads up to the attic, and Sébastien proceeds one floor up. A narrow door opens into the top space of the house. The two small windows, where presently soft raindrops fall upon, allow sufficient light in as he strolls along. The loft is a large space, and he notices some trunks in the middle of it. With a hard pull he opens one and sees it has books inside it. He takes out a few, and he recognises them as his father's who, in his rare free moments, loved to read, choosing quiet spots around the house to do so. He puts the books back and opens the other trunk. Clothes emerge. When he picks up a dress, Sébastien feels a shock go through his body when he realises the clothes belonged to his deceased wife. He drops the dress and slams the trunk shut before he stands up. Then, slowly, he turns and kneels down again. A slip of the fabric is caught in the lid of the trunk. He opens the trunk and pulls out the dress he was holding only moments before. Natalie used to wear it to parties that they sometimes went to. A few more dresses emerge, and skirts and blouses. He never realised she had so many pretty clothes. Reaching the bottom of the trunk, he sees clothing he remembers her wearing most of the time. Her riding pants. He holds a pair and strokes it. Then, with a sigh and a feeling of sadness, he puts all the items back and takes his time closing the lid. He stands up and takes another look around the attic before descending, back to the first floor, along the landing, and down the staircase that leads to the kitchen. The men have gone, and he hears them outside where the rain has now stopped and the sun has chased away the clouds.

'I'm going into town now,' Sébastien tells them. 'Can I give someone a ride?' he offers. They decline and take their own means of transport back to their homes. Sébastien gets into his car and with a brief honk of the horn he leaves the men and the house behind.

After a pleasant ride through scenery that is refreshed by the rain shower, Sébastien turns his car into the parking area at the hospital. He jumps out and, about to close the car door, he is surprised to see his sister-in-law leaving through the front exit of the hospital. She doesn't notice him, and he decides to leave it at that. He watches her as she gets into her car and drives away.

A few minutes later he is in his brother's room, wondering how he feels after his wife's visit.

'François, how are you doing?' he greets his brother

who looks at him with a dull glance. The bandage around his head has been changed. A large adhesive plaster now covers the head wound.

'Louise was here,' he says. He reaches out and takes a large envelop from his bedside stand. 'Divorce papers, that's what she came for. To deliver them personally. Afraid they might go astray,' he adds with sarcasm in his voice. Sébastien sits down on the side of the bed. 'She may also have come to see how you were,' he tries to smooth over the situation.

François looks at him. 'You don't believe that yourself,' he says.

'But, why now?' Sébastien wonders. 'It's a bit callous.'

'Well, I've realised that she's always been like that,' François says. 'I've had a lot of time to think about our marriage, while lying here. How ironic. And it has always been about her.' He looks up at Sébastien. 'I suppose I was the only one who never saw that.'

'Your children?' Sébastien asks. 'Do they know?'

'Like I said, I was the last one to know. Blind. Love makes blind. Damn cliché.'

'Do your children know about the divorce?' Sébastien clarifies his question.

François shrugs the question aside. 'I haven't a clue. But I suppose, they too saw this coming. Besides, they're at college. They're not home a lot any more. And George is in Lyon.'

He drops his head back into his pillow. 'I'm rather tired now, Sébastien. Would you mind?'

'Sure. You rest. Do you know when you can come home?' François closes his eyes and remains silent. 'OK, I'll see you tomorrow then,' Sébastien says. He rises from the bed and leaves the room.

In the corridor he stops a nurse. 'Can you check on my brother a bit more often?' he asks of her. 'He just had some bad news.'

The nurse gives him a friendly nod. 'Of course.'

At La Fontenelle Sébastien wanders about the stables, but the boxes are empty. Most of the horses are training, and the rest are in the fields around the property. He walks along the path leading up to the training track and he soon spots his father and the horse trainer in its centre by the fencing. Sébastien watches the horses' supple gallop, the dull thuds of the hooves hitting sand, and their sweaty skins shining in the sun. He waits until the horses, with the jockeys on their backs, have raced passed him and then makes his way across the track, ducks underneath the fence and into the safety of the centre. His father is concentrating on the horses and watches their progress intently, now and then discussing something with the trainer. This is how he remembers his father best, mostly busy with the horses, wearing his riding pants. Although in recent years he no longer rides as often as he used to.

'Papa. How is it going?'

'Well, see for yourself,' Pierre replies. 'Do you see that black stallion? He wasn't named Flaming Star for nothing!'

Sébastien observes the horse racing in front of the rest and gaining ground at a fiery speed. 'He sure is a remarkable horse, Papa.'

'He's still young, but he has won a few races already,' Pierre says. 'Who does that remind you of, son.'

'Monseigneur?' Sébastien guesses.

His father looks at him with a smile on his face. 'Monseigneur,' he affirms. 'Did you know he lived to a ripe old age? Died here, at Fontenelle.'

It pleases Sébastien that the horses still give his father so much enjoyment. Retirement or not. 'Papa, I just came back from the hospital – '

'How's François,' his father interrupts.

'Getting better, but, he had some bad news. Louise came by to drop off divorce papers.'

For a moment Pierre's eyes are not on the racing horses but on Sébastien. 'That's a bit callous of that woman,' he says.

'My thoughts exactly. But you know how he loved her.'

Pierre shakes his head. 'That is something I've never understood. Well, he will be a lot better off without her.' He turns his gaze towards the horses once again, and a contented look appears on his face. 'Does Sylvia know?' he then asks.

Sébastien shrugs his shoulders. 'I'm sure she'll find out soon.' He also turns his face towards the racing horses, and it fills him with joy, seeing the animals in a brisk gallop moving along the track. A feeling he couldn't have imagined possible only a few weeks ago.

The horses come to a halt, their nostrils snorting wildly, foam around their mouths, and their sweaty skins quivering. The trainer decides it has been enough, and the jockeys come down from their horses to lead them back to the stables. Pierre and Sébastien follow in their wake, and soon enter the yard where Thomas is already awaiting their return. He spots his grandfather and runs towards him. 'Grandpapa, can I ride now?'

'Not today, Thomas. Tomorrow you'll be the first. We'll go over to Les Jonquières and then you can ride your pony.'

Thomas grabs his grandfather's hand as Pierre addresses Sébastien. 'Careful, son. I don't need to remind you of how Cécile feels about this.'

'Papa, he is with me when he rides. I'll make sure no harm comes to him.'

'I know you were always a bit annoyed with Cécile for not wanting to ride. I hope these riding lessons you're giving Thomas are not out of a need to prove something.'

'It's Thomas,' Sébastien rationalises. 'He *wants* to ride.'

Apart from the meaningful look his father gives him, nothing else is said about the matter.

Ever since he had overheard a conversation when his mother phoned Sylvia, Thomas has been walking around with discontent on his little face. Sylvia had tried to cheer up Thomas, who knew that his mother's insistence not to let him ride a horse was interfering with the lessons he was receiving from his grandpapa, which was a secret that should have remained so. 'But I *want* to ride the horses,' had been his stubborn reaction after his great-grandmother had relayed the advice. 'But your maman doesn't want you to. It's too dangerous.' To which Thomas had angrily sat down in a large armchair and folded his arms. Sylvia couldn't help but think that she had sometimes seen the same stubborn sullenness in Sébastien's face when he was young.

Currently, Sylvia attempts to get the boy to go outside and accompany her to the stables. 'Thomas, why won't you come? You adore the horses!'

The look on her great-grandson's face makes her feel guilty. 'You know how your mother feels about this, Thomas. Your grand-mère and now uncle François … Do you understand why your maman is worried about you riding?'

Thomas bites his lip, but then, reluctantly, slides out

of the large armchair. He solemnly passes Sylvia, and they walk out of the house, across the yard, and in the direction of the stables. Some of the jockeys are just returning from their morning training, and Thomas has suddenly forgotten all about his mother's prohibition. He runs ahead of Sylvia and asks one of the jockeys if he can take the horse to his box. The man is obliging and smilingly hands him the reins. Happy with the task, Thomas leads the horse inside and begins to wipe him dry, even though he can only reach as high as the legs. One of the stable hands assists him and wipes the horse's back.

Sylvia looks around for one of the older mares she usually rides, but finds the horse has been put in the field. She asks a stable hand to help her with the saddle and gear, and they walk towards the fence. When Thomas sees her, he runs after her to the field. 'Grand-mère!'

Sylvia watches the horse she's been calling, ambling towards the gate, which she now opens to saddle her up. Thomas has reached the fence as well and is about to climb it when Sylvia stops him. 'Thomas, I thought you wanted to look after the race horses?'

'Can I ride with you?' the boy asks.

'No, Thomas. You know what your maman has said,' she replies as she straps the saddle on her horse. 'Go and find Sébastien, maybe you can go with him to Les Jonquières.'

The boy's face lights up. '*D'accord*,' he says and storms off towards the house while Sylvia mounts her horse and rides off in the direction of the forest, with her long greying hair waving in the wind.

Jeanette looks up when Thomas storms into the kitchen. 'Where's Grandpapa?' he asks.

Jeanette points towards the forecourt. 'He's just about to leave.' With the same speed that he entered with,

Thomas now runs outside to see his grandpapa's car drive off.

From the corner of his eye Sébastien notices the boy in his rear-view mirror and he hesitates but then stops. Thomas is soon by the driver's side of the car. 'Grandpapa, can I come with you?'

Sébastien is somewhat reluctant but agrees. 'But you know what your maman has said,' he reminds Thomas. 'I cannot let you ride.'

Thomas walks around the car and gets in. Sébastien helps him click the seatbelt in place, and they drive off.

'But you promised yesterday,' Thomas whines. 'Yesterday, you said, I could ride my pony.'

'That was before your mother called, Thomas. And I don't want to annoy her.'

Thomas looks at him with a sullen expression. 'You said, it was our secret. That no one needs to know.'

'I did,' is all Sébastien says. He looks at the scenery that passes by the car window. 'Maybe the big white dog will be there, *hein*,' he tries to cheer up his grandson. Briefly, Thomas's face brightens, only to cloud over again.

Before long they drive up the unpaved road towards the house and stables at Les Jonquières. Sébastien notices the contractor, accompanied by the other men, talking to Nicolas. Thomas jumps out of the car and goes into the stables as Sébastien joins the men. 'Bonjour,' he says.

'Monsieur Maréchal,' the contractor greets him. 'I've drawn up the plan for that corner stable. Maybe we can have a look at it?'

Once inside the house, the contractor spreads out the plans on the kitchen table. It's a simple, straightforward drawing of the stable block showing the part that is to be mended. 'And I thought, maybe we can extend it, so you can have a few more horses,' the builder explains while pointing at the drawing. Sébastien nods in agreement. 'Good idea.'

'Here's a list of the materials we need,' the contractor says. 'If you could order those. But, I could get you a deal if I order it for you.'

'Very well. You order the materials,' Sébastien says. Nicolas pulls out a bottle of wine as Sébastien takes a few glasses from the counter, and the men sit down to have a drink. While they are busy talking about the new addition to the stable block, the door is opened abruptly and Julien appears. 'Fire!' he screams. 'There's a fire in the stables!'

Sébastien shoots up from his chair. 'Call the fire brigade!' he calls out and runs outside followed by the others. In the yard, they see smoke seeping through the open stable door, and curling along the wall where it is dispersed by the breeze outside.

'*Mon Dieu*, not again,' Raymond utters.

Sébastien rushes into the stable block where he is confronted by the flames. 'Thomas! Thomas!' The heat is intense, and Sébastien has to retreat.

The men are entering with buckets of water and start throwing it on the pile of burning material. 'My grandson!' Sébastien yells. 'My grandson is in here!'

'Damn!' Nicolas starts looking about him. 'Thomas! Where are you!' More buckets of water are carried in by the men, and they throw the water on the fast-burning flames that have now caught the bales of straw that are piled up at the side. 'Thomas!' Sébastien tries to fight his way around the fire but the flames keep shooting up. 'Thomas!'

'More water here!' Nicolas calls out as he, too, tries to find a way around the burning area. As the men throw more buckets of water on the fire, the flames sizzle and smoke, and Sébastien sees a chance to get past the fire. 'Thomas!' The violent smoke in the stable block prevents him from breathing properly, and he pulls his shirt over his nose to avoid inhaling the fumes. The men keep throwing water on the burning bales of straw, and the smoke intensifies as the flames are smothered by the water.

Outside, the sound of the siren of a fire engine comes their way as it speeds towards the house.

'Thomas!' Sébastien cries desperately but there is still no sign of the boy.

'He must've inhaled the smoke, maybe he's lying here somewhere.' Nicolas's remark only brings more despair to Sébastien who jerks at every stall door in this part of the stable but there is no sign of the boy.

'Are you sure he was in here?' Nicolas wonders. Through the receding smoke they go outside where the firemen have just pulled out the hoses.

Among all the commotion in the yard the large white dog appears. Beside him is Thomas, who looks on with great interest. 'Grandpapa, what is happening?' Sébastien turns around and grabs the boy by his shoulders. 'Thomas! Thank God you're alright,' He almost smothers the boy with his embrace. 'Where were you?'

Thomas is unaware of what has happened only moments before. 'The nice dog was here, and we went to the field to play.'

Sébastien lifts his grandson up off the ground and hugs him. 'Thank God.'

While the firemen enter the stable block to establish if the fire is fully extinguished, the fire commander approaches Sébastien. 'Can we have a talk, monsieur.'

'*Bien sûr.*' Still holding Thomas, Sébastien shows the commander to the house, and they enter. The large white dog slips between their legs and goes inside, too. 'Better stay here for now, Thomas,' Sébastien tells his grandson as he lowers him to the floor.

'This is the second time we've had to come here, monsieur,' the commander says. 'Did you have any flammable material in that stable?'

'There is always something that can burn,' Sébastien replies, stoically.

'Yes. I've heard you're working on those stable blocks. Maybe one of the men forgot to switch off a tool of some kind?'

'Unlikely.'

'Wiring? Have you had that checked?'

'The fire was on the ground, monsieur. It's solid concrete,' Sébastien says.

'*Bien*,' the commander says and walks to the door.

'Maybe you should talk to Julien,' Sébastien suggests. 'He was outside, he came in to warn us.'

They proceed to walk outside and Thomas grabs his grandfather's hand. Together they walk over to the rest of the men.

Inside the stable, firemen have taken the straw bales apart to make sure there are no smouldering sparks lingering inside the bales. A strangely shaped soot mark has remained on the ground. The smell of smoke still lingers heavily in the air, and the ceiling is blackened. 'Another clean-up job,' Sébastien hears Nicolas say behind him. 'And just when we were finished in here.'

'*Oui*. A thorough clean,' Sébastien concurs. 'Otherwise, no horse would want to be in here.'

Thomas pulls up his nose. '*Drôle d'odeur.*'

In the yard, Sébastien sees the fire commander and Julien talk to each other. 'Let's have a look at your pony,' he proposes, as a means of removing his grandson from the site. He leads the boy to the paddock where the pony is grazing. As Sébastien leans on the fence, Thomas crawls underneath it and runs towards the animal. Thomas reaches out to pet his pony on the shoulder, and looks in the direction of his grandfather with a question burning on his lips, but he just smiles.

The sight of the boy playing with his pony, as if he never knew anything else, brings to mind the promise he has made to Thomas, but dubiety restricts him. His daughter's refusal to allow Thomas to ride undermines that promise, and it puts him in an uncomfortable position.

At the far end of the field Sébastien sees a police car approach. He turns to see the firemen clearing their gear away and preparing to leave. 'Thomas!' he calls out. 'Thomas, come. We need to go.'

With some hesitation Thomas comes towards him. 'It's lunchtime too,' his grandfather says. 'Aren't you hungry?' Thomas follows him across the yard where the police car has just pulled up. Sébastien tells Thomas to go with Nicolas, 'he'll give you something to eat,' before he shows the police around the fire damaged stable.

The police officers glance into the stable block, and one of them takes a few photos. 'Why did you leave inflammable material in the middle of this stable block?' the other asks Sébastien.

'We didn't,' the latter replies. 'All was clear, and we had only just received those bales of straw. We use that to cover the ground in the boxes.'

'So, that caught fire?'

'No. A pile of rubbish,' and Sébastien points to the sooty spot on the ground, 'was set alight.'

'*Bien*, monsieur Maréchal. This is the second time you claim someone else has set fire to your property.'

'What do you mean, *claim*? It was set alight. And you

still have failed to come up with the culprit who was responsible for the previous fire.'

'We need evidence, monsieur, and we haven't found any.'

Sébastien starts to feel frustrated. 'Well, look for it then!' He is about to turn and go back to the house. 'I thought the police had a forensic department. Get them to search this place!'

Sébastien begins to walk towards the house, and the police officer follows him close behind. 'Monsieur Maréchal, please. We have to look at all the options. You can't just accuse people.'

Sébastien faces him. 'But you can accuse *me*?' His face has turned to anger. 'My grandson could have been killed in there! And you're just sitting behind your desks filing papers instead of searching for arsonists!'

'Sorry, was your grandson in there? Wouldn't it be possible that – '

'Don't you dare accuse my grandson!' He points a warning finger at the police officer. 'He was out in the field, playing, as it happens. Nowhere near the fire!'

'Calm down, monsieur. No one is accusing anybody.'

'*You* are!'

The police officer looks at Sébastien. 'Is it possible to talk to the boy?'

'No!'

Sébastien strides over to the kitchen door and enters. Inside, the atmosphere is more tranquil than what he just left behind outside. The men sit around the table with Thomas in their midst, eating their lunch. Sébastien takes a deep breath, walks over to the sink and pours a glass of water. He gulps it down in one go.

'Patron,' Nicolas says. 'Sit down. Have something to eat.'

'Nothing goes on an empty stomach,' Julien says.

Sébastien strokes his grandson's hair and sits down. 'Thomas. Thomas, can you tell us what happened when we arrived and you got out of the car and walked into the stables?'

Surprised faces turn his way. '*Mais* … Patron.' Sébastien refrains from acknowledging their objections and addresses his grandson once more. 'Thomas, can you tell us?'

The boy puts his slice of bread down. '*Mais oui!*' he enthusiastically starts. 'I walked inside and there was nothing there. Only a man. And then I saw the dog. He was in the hay at the back. And I called him, and then we went outside and we played in the field!'

'What man?'

Thomas looks around the table. 'A man.'

'Anyone in this room?'

Nicolas intervenes. 'I think you should hear what Julien has to say, patron.'

'It was me, patron,' Julien says. 'And I saw Thomas leave with the dog.'

'And?'

'He went to the field, and that's where he has been playing with the dog. Oh, and I went to the back of the stable, then I realised that the eroded wall was in the other stable block so I went there. I didn't see anyone in the yard so I assumed you were all at that stable block.'

Sébastien listens intently.

'And when I didn't see any of you guys there, I walked back and saw smoke coming from the stable.' He pulls out his phone. 'And I saw a strange car drive away along the forest road.' Julien shows them the photo he took of the intruder before he had rushed to the house to warn the others.

'Did you tell the fire commander?' Sébastien wants to know.

'Yes. Showed him the photo too.'

Sébastien frowns. 'Then why didn't they let the police know? ... Are they still here?' They listen as a car drives away. 'No,' Nicolas confirms.

'Julien, we have to go to the police station with this.'

Julien makes an apologetic gesture. 'Patron, let's finish our lunch first, *hein*. Nothing goes on an empty stomach.'

Raymond slaps Julien on his shoulder, and the others, too, can't suppress their laughter for Julien's favourite preoccupation, and they continue their respite.

The police officer who is sitting across from them has been on the phone for the past five minutes, and Sébastien wonders if she's interested in their statements at all. He looks at Julien who is sitting next to him with a tiresome expression on his face. The latter stands up and starts pacing up and down the room.

'Messieurs,' the police officer finally says, putting the phone down. 'Where were we?'

Julien takes his seat again as Sébastien is about to tell her the rest of this morning's events.

'The fire on your property,' she continues. 'We are waiting for the report from the fire department. When we've received that, we can continue our investigation. Is there anything else?'

'Well, the photo Julien took,' Sébastien says. 'Are you not interested in the photo?'

'We don't know what that has to do with our research,' the police officer says.

For a moment Sébastien's glare is locked on the woman's face, then, abruptly, he stands up. 'Right,' he says. 'Sorry we've taken up so much of your time,' and he strides out of the office with Julien close behind.

'Patron. Patron, don't you want to give her the photo I took?'

'Julien, they hardly show interest. I have no patience for this lax attitude.' He pushes the door open, and they walk outside. 'And something else came to my mind.'

He opens the car doors for them to get into the car. Sébastien rummages in the glove compartment, and finds what he is looking for. 'This is the phone number of the person who cancelled my order of timber a while ago. I thought, if we make a printout of your photo, and hand it in with this number, maybe, hopefully, the police will be a bit more forthcoming.'

He turns the key in the ignition, starts the engine, and they speed off.

6

*A*fter having collected his brother from the hospital and delivered him to his parents' house, Sébastien currently rides one of his father's young racehorses along the forest path on the way to the beach. Disturbing thoughts about the arson attacks on his property occupy his mind and prevent him from enjoying the attractive scenery that surrounds La Fontenelle. He enters the sandy area and looks across the beach and the blue Mediterranean Sea before he urges the horse into a full gallop. Along the water's edge where the sand is firmer and seawater splashes up, the horse seems to be in full control. It makes Sébastien aware of the potential of this animal, and he pushes him even faster. The horse almost rears when they reach the forested area at the other end of the beach. Sébastien pets the animal on his neck, and then decides to take a right turn, off the beach and onto the path that leads to Les Jonquières. The horse picks up speed again and races through the woods, across the grassy divide, past the Fairy Tree and on to the domain of Les Jonquières.

When he enters the yard, he sees the men by the side of the stable block where part of the wall needs to be replaced. He jumps off his horse and slings the reins over a branch of a tree. The contractor is just instructing the men as he approaches them, and he notices the stall with a gaping hole where the wall has been broken away.

'Morning, monsieur Maréchal,' the contractor greets him, and Sébastien starts to inspect the progress. 'How long do you think it'll take before it's finished?' he asks.

'We have all the materials, a few days is my guess.

No more,' is his reply.

'Patron!' They turn their heads when Julien approaches in a somewhat agitated manner. 'Patron, I just had a call from the police department. I think we should go there!'

'Now?' Sébastien looks over at his horse, who is waiting patiently while resting a hind leg and enjoying the shade. Julien nods. 'I think it's best. Melt the iron while it's hot.'

'Sorry?'

'I mean, they came up with some information, and maybe if we go there now, they might speed things up,' Julien clarifies. 'You know I gave them my photo,' he adds with some pride.

'OK. But I don't have my car here. We'll have to take yours.'

Sébastien casts a glance towards his horse as he begins to follow Julien. 'Can someone look after my horse, please,' he calls over his shoulder.

They get into the old Deux Chevaux that Julien is driving, and soon the wheels hit the dirt road. The car is not exactly equipped with a modern shock-absorber system, and Sébastien finds himself being tossed back and forth. He looks over at Julien but it doesn't seem to bother him at all. 'Ever thought about buying a more modern version of this car?' Sébastien endeavours.

'Why? This one works fine. Belonged to my father,' Julien informs him. 'Never gives me much trouble.' The final jolt lands them onto the paved road, and they drive on in the direction of Nice.

'Aren't we going the wrong way?' Sébastien attempts. 'Shouldn't we be in the village?'

'No, they're letting Nice solve it. Maybe rightly so, they seem to be better equipped over there.' Julien accelerates and the little Deux Chevaux's purr becomes a roar, which is an indication for Sébastien to sit the ride out as talking would be a loud affair.

On the outskirts of Nice, Julien takes the direction to the relevant police station. He knows the city by heart, and before long Julien parks the Deux Chevaux in front of the *Police Municipale* from where he was contacted from earlier. The sun burns hard on the pavement, but soon they find themselves inside the air-conditioned building. Julien enquires at reception where to find the police officer who informed him of the arson-case investigation. Sébastien looks about him in this pleasant building, a remnant of 'old school' architecture. Fortunately, this building has been preserved and is now in use as a police station. Meanwhile, Julien has learned that the police officer they came to see is in the building, and they sit down on a bench by the wall to wait for him. After a while, the policeman they intent on talking to appears. 'Julien Laroche?'

'*Oui.*' Julien jumps up. 'And this is monsieur Maréchal.'

The police officer looks at both before informing them. 'I'm sorry, but the photo you sent was of a car that was reported stolen – '

'*Mais* … this morning you said you had a breakthrough!' Julien is surprised but annoyed at the same time.

'I'm sorry, but I might've been a bit too hasty with that information. Just an hour ago we had a report from the Languedoc police. That car in your photo was stolen last week in Montpellier.'

'*Zut alors …* '

'I assume you are looking for this stolen car?' Sébastien says. 'To establish who was driving it through the woods around Les Jonquières?'

The police officer looks at him decisively. 'We are.'

'And the number?' Julien asks.

'What number?'

'The telephone number,' Sébastien says.

'Oh, yes. That too. The owner left his phone in the car, so that was stolen too. They must have used the phone to make the call, so it could not be traced back to them.'

Disappointment slides across Sébastien's face, and Julien feels he could sink through the floor because of this setback.

'I am sorry, *messieurs*,' the police officer apologises. 'Now if you will excuse me? There is a load of unsolved cases on my desk.'

Sébastien starts walking to the exit. 'Let's go,' he mumbles under his breath.

'Well, it was worth a try,' Julien reasons. '*Retour à la case départ.*'

While they enter the heat outside, Sébastien stops for a moment. 'There's only one person I know of who doesn't want me to be at Les Jonquières,' he says. 'That Morgan fellow.'

Julien makes a demeaning gesture with his hand. '*Le criminel.*'

'Why would you say that?'

'Because it's criminal, patron! Criminal to want to destroy the scenery in an area where *we* live!' Sweat starts pearling on his forehead. 'The whole village thinks so,' he adds as they cross the street and walk over to the Deux Chevaux, 'and I've heard some strange stories going about, patron.'

'If you want,' Pierre addresses Sébastien, 'I know a man who can find out for you. He's a private investigator,

I've known him for years.' They are in the stables at La Fontenelle where the horses are just returning from their training. Sébastien fills a few troughs with feed as he ponders his father's remark. 'A detective?'

'He calls himself a private investigator,' is Pierre's reply. 'We went to school together. He lives in Marseille. I can call him if you want.' He has just finished drying the face of one of the horses and is stroking the animal on his neck.

'Do you think it's necessary?' Sébastien says.

'Well, don't you want this solved?' Pierre prompts. 'Remember, if the police remain so slack, it could happen again.'

Sébastien empties the remainder of the feed from the bucket into a trough. 'I prefer to wait for the police report. We've now given them some clues.'

Pierre sighs, shaking his head. 'Well … If you've made up your mind, let me know.' He grabs a currycomb and begins combing another horse. While Sébastien puts the bucket back, he catches a glimpse of his stepmother riding her horse along the forest path towards the stables. In front of her in the saddle, is Thomas. Sébastien nudges his father, who now notices them as well.

'Not Sylvia too,' Pierre mumbles. '*Bien* … it's out of my hands now. There is no point in objecting to the boy riding a horse.'

Sébastien's thoughts wander back to the years when it was he himself who sat in front of Sylvia in the saddle. He was only nine years old then, and had just started living at Les Jonquières when he had met his soon to be stepmother on the beach.

Sylvia enters the yard, and Sébastien walks towards them to lift Thomas from the saddle. 'I rode with Grand-mère!' he says enthusiastically.

'Lovely,' his grandfather says, at the same time looking up at his stepmother with questioning eyes.

Sylvia slides out of the saddle. 'He was fine, Sébastien. And I have to confess, you were right when you said that there's no way for him to avoid the horses when they're constantly around him.' She smiles and leads her horse to her box. 'Do you want to help me, Thomas?' The boy has already taken a towel to wipe the horse dry. '*Bien sûr,*' he says and walks into the box as well.

With a cupped hand, Sébastien takes a few sips of water from the tap before he leaves the yard to make his way over to the house. He enters by the kitchen door and finds his brother at the other end walking in from the hall. 'Hello, François! How are you feeling?'

His brother appears to have just rolled out of bed, wearing a crumpled T-shirt and shorts. 'Ah, Sébastien.' He takes a glass of Jeanette's home-made lemon juice before he turns to face his brother. 'Sébastien. I want to ask you a favour.'

Sébastien looks at him in earnest. 'Sure.'

'Would you mind driving me to my house tomorrow?'

'Tomorrow? But, I thought you wanted to stay home for a while? To convalesce?'

François lowers himself onto one of the chairs at the kitchen table. 'No, I think it's best I go as soon as I can. I want to sort this divorce business with my lawyer.' He looks up at Sébastien. 'Some things you just cannot do over the phone.'

Sébastien takes a seat opposite his brother. 'Fine, I'll take you. But who will look after you when you're in Marseille? If Louise is not there – '

'I'm not sure where she is,' François bluntly interrupts him, 'but it's highly unlikely she would've helped … No, Louise is not the nursing type,' he adds wryly. 'I'm feeling better, Sébastien. I'll manage.'

The morning air is growing warmer, and birds are chirping noisily in the tree tops around the property when Sébastien waits by his car while François is saying goodbye to his mother and father. Little Thomas stands between them, shuffling his feet somewhat impatiently on the gravel. François pats the boy on his head before joining Sébastien and getting into the car, too. With a brief honk of the horn they drive off. Sylvia waves to her departing sons and is the last one to turn and walk back to the house once the car has disappeared behind the trees. Sébastien steers the vehicle onto the main road and makes his way to the A8 motorway for the shortest drive to Marseille. The warmth of the summer weather remains drifting in the air, with a few white clouds hovering above in the blue sky, casting odd shadows across the landscape.

About fifteen minutes from the boundaries of the city of Marseille, Sébastien takes a turn to drive in a more southerly direction before entering the town closer to its centre. The slow pace of other cars obliges them to adjust their speed. On the way, François has informed Sébastien that he would like him to drive to his lawyer's office, and currently they're searching for the building that is situated not far from the city centre. The tall, somewhat tired looking buildings, are casting shade onto the narrow streets. There where the roads catch more sun, the glare shines right on them. Traffic is slow and soon the reason becomes clear. Roadworks obstruct the thoroughfare and a temporary traffic light that emits a burning red, stops them from continuing on their way. Sébastien looks about him and at the street ahead but his view is blocked by roadwork machinery.

'Marseille is never finished either,' François sighs.

'Roads become worn and need repairing, François.'

'Not this one. Look, they're replacing the sewerage.' He looks behind him. 'This could take a while, Sébastien. Isn't there a way out of this traffic?'

Sébastien, too, looks around for ways to escape from the line of cars and find a different route. He looks towards the pavement and notices not many pedestrians there; it might give them an opportunity to bend the rules a bit. Then his eyes are drawn to a man he once had an unpleasant encounter with in Café Villeneuve. He looks more closely at the balding man in his mid-fifties, sitting at a roadside café discussing something with another man sitting beside him. 'François, look.' His brother casts a brief glance towards the small restaurant.

'That's that Morgan fellow.'

'Who?'

'Morgan. That man who wanted to buy Les Jonquières. The one who threatened Papa and me.'

'He threatened you?' François now has a closer look as well. 'He doesn't look like a forbidding person.'

'Well, let me tell you, he has a big mouth.' Sébastien searches his pockets for his phone and whips it out. Within seconds he aims the camera function at the man, who is sitting quite unaware at the café table.

'You're not taking his picture,' François says, sceptically.

'Proof is what we need,' Sébastien replies a few clicks later.

'What is *that* going to prove? He's just sitting there having a coffee with a friend!' François shakes his head. 'You're becoming too paranoid.'

Sébastien has another good look of the men sipping their coffees.

'Green!' François calls out.

'What?'

'The light just went green.' Impatient honking accompanies his words and Sébastien quickly puts his car in gear to steer around the road blockade. Once passed it, he resumes driving at the allowed speed. They continue along the road, passing streets left and right until they notice the street where the lawyers' office is situated, and Sébastien turns off. 'There's a parking garage at the other end,' François says, and Sébastien steers towards it through the street, past the lawyers' building.

After they have circled around the large parking garage for a few minutes, they find a spot to park the car.

'That's fine.' François grabs his briefcase from the backseat, and they leave the car park to walk to the lawyers' office.

Inside the building, the cool air in the lobby is a welcome change from Sébastien's warm car. At the reception desk, François enquires after his lawyer, and then enters the elevator to go up, leaving his brother in the spacious cool lobby. Sébastien sits down in a waiting area where an aquarium radiates a peaceful sentiment. He takes out his phone and looks for the photos he just took, examining the images closely and he concludes that there can be no mistake. It is Morgan. He remembers the strange mole he had on his chin, which is also clearly visible in the photos. Sébastien has no recollection of ever having seen the man who sits beside Morgan. Maybe his brother is right. He might have just been sitting there having a coffee with a friend. What does he actually know about the man? Maybe he lives here.

Sébastien stands up and slowly paces up and down the lobby, watching people enter and leave the building. His thoughts suddenly turn to his daughter Cécile who moved to Marseille two years previously, to start her new job as a fitness instructor. It was about the same time that he and Angéline separated.

Forty minutes after he entered the elevator, his brother now appears in the lobby. 'Sébastien, let's go to my house. I've just learned that Louise is not there. Otherwise, a hotel might've been more appropriate.'

Sébastien follows his brother into the warmth outside, and they stroll over to the parking garage to collect the car. 'Do you have your bankcard at the ready?' François alludes to paying the parking.

A short while later, they are on their way to François's house who lives on the outskirts, more to the south of the city, near the university where he teaches when he is not engaged in his oceanographic research.

'Have you made any settlements?' Sébastien asks his brother who casts a trying look out the car window.

'Signed some papers … I suppose things have to be sold because there is not much money left.'

'Louise instigated it, François.'

'The house has to be sold. Louise has demanded half of its value,' François is hesitant to say.

'She's got a nerve,' Sébastien reacts. 'Where are your children going to live when they come home?'

'George has his flat in Lyon. But Madeleine, she's not eighteen, still lives at home when she's not at the *lycée*.' François blows out a gasp of air. 'It's a mess.'

Sébastien steers the car into the street where his brother lives. A few moments later the striking house with its blue shutters comes into view. It's partly hidden by the wall that surrounds the house. François gets out of the car, and opens the wrought iron gate, painted in Provence blue, to allow Sébastien to drive his car onto the paved area that once was part of the garden. He parks in the shade of the only tree there. They have barely arrived, when a teenage girl comes running around the house and towards them. 'Papa! Papa, how are you?' Madeleine embraces her father. 'Mummy didn't even tell us you were in hospital!'

'I'm … better now,' is her father's surprised reply.

'But, I thought you were at school?!'

'Papa. Is it true? About you and Mummy?'

François takes his daughter by the hand. 'Let's go inside. We'll talk there.'

Sébastien opens the boot of his car and removes François's bag to then follow the other two into the house. He finds his niece crying on the sofa as his brother is sitting next to her, trying to explain the situation. Sébastien continues into the kitchen and opens a few cupboards in search of coffee. He notices the coffee machine on the counter.

'I won't! I won't live with her!' he hears Madeleine cry from the other room. 'I'll find my own place, Papa!'

'You can still live with me. Just, it will be smaller, you understand.'

Sébastien has managed the workings of his brother's state-of-the art coffee machine and holds a cup underneath to catch the brown, hot liquid. The ice-cube maker in the fridge provides him with a few ice-cubes that he drops into his coffee to make it instantly drinkable. He finds that the bread in the bread bin is still edible and he looks for something in the fridge to spread on it. With his meagre lunch in hand, he finds a seat on the patio, just outside the kitchen door. Birds sing in the bushes around the garden, where the flower borders look bleak, overgrown, and tangled, and the lawn is in grave need of mowing. While chewing on the piece of crumbly bread, Sébastien hears muffled voices through the open kitchen door, and he establishes that François has calmed his daughter to a certain extent. Sometime later he hears them in the kitchen and François appears in the door. 'Do you want something to eat?' he asks. 'There isn't much there, but I can open a tin of something.'

Sébastien looks his way. 'I think I'd better go back, François. I see you have enough on your mind.' He stands up and follows his brother into the house. '*Bien,*' the latter says. 'Thank you for driving me back. Appreciate it.'

Madeleine looks at her uncle, remnants of tears still show in the girl's face. 'Uncle Sébastien. Please, send Granny and Granddad my love.'

The two brothers enter the hall. 'I'll collect my car when I can,' François says. 'I still have an old vehicle sitting in the garage that I can use.'

The men embrace, and Sébastien takes his seat behind the wheel. 'Look after yourself, François. And if you need *any*thing, don't hesitate to ask.'

François nods and closes the car door. With a wave of his hand, he makes his way back into the house.

Instead of going back by the fastest route, Sébastien deflects in an easterly direction and finds himself on a more quiet road near the south coast. The sky is now stark blue above and the sun burns harshly on the bonnet. Sébastien closes the windows of the Citroën and turns up the air-conditioning. The faded green in the rocky banks on either side of the road accompanies him and after a while, a town comes into view, Saint-Cyr-sur-Mer, the town where his ex-wife hails from. She didn't remain here but left for Paris when she had outgrown her teenage years. It was there where they met some sixteen years ago.

Since they celebrated their wedding here, he hasn't been back this way. Angéline's only surviving parent moved from here shortly afterwards.

He follows the road until he exits the town on the other side. When he reaches Toulon, he decides on driving north to connect with the road he rejected earlier. The landscape is more level here, with to his left, infrequent peaks reaching for the skies. The expanse of the broad sky stretches far in front of him, where now wisps of white cloud break the clear blue atmosphere. Here and there green trees on both sides of the four-lane road fade into the landscape to give way to greyish green banks that sweep up and hide the vine culture beyond. He realises once more that this is what he has been missing all the years he has spent in Paris. He is a child of nature, always has been. When he was a young boy, he endlessly roamed through the mountains, hopping from one rock to the next like a mountain goat, spotting birds and other wildlife. Always with his large white dog Belle, and often accompanied by the wise mountain man César, the one who took him in when his mother had died in childbirth. César was the one, too, who curbed his unruliness. He often came home to a surly Angelina, his adoptive big sister, who reprimanded him for his dirty clothes and giving her extra work. He smiles as he thinks of her, and her brother Jean; he does love them. They're now retired and are still living in Canada. And after he came to live with his father, the countless hours he spent in the forests around Les Jonquières and on the beach. He stayed in that natural environment when he had started a family of his own.

A few more towns interrupt the scenery until the four-lane road gives way to a six-lane road, and he presses on in the direction of La Fontenelle, which is about twenty minutes outside Nice. A sudden urge compels him to speed up, and return to the land he has always loved and where he feels he belongs. He ponders his father's suggestion about the private investigator, as the police haven't been expeditious in solving his problems with the arson attacks.

When the landscape becomes more forested, an indication that he is nearing home, he turns off into the narrow road leading to La Fontenelle, and before long he parks his car in its court, next to a familiar green Renault. After the long drive, he feels weary and walks towards the kitchen door with a feeling of apprehension, wondering what possessed Angéline to come for a visit. As he opens the door, he hears voices coming from the front room, interspersed with the high, objecting, voice of Thomas. He allows for a slower pace when hearing the passionate conversation and he inquisitively finds his way through the hall and into the room. Faces turn his way and he greets Sylvia and Angéline as Thomas runs towards him and pulls his hand. 'I want to stay!' he cries. Sébastien lifts the boy off the ground, and into his arms as he turns a questioning face towards the two women.

'Hello Sébastien,' Angéline says. 'Good to see you.'

Sylvia looks at him somewhat apologetically. 'Angéline has instructions to take Thomas back to Paris with her,' she simply says.

'Instructions? What is this, the child protection police?'

Angéline approaches him and reaches to take Thomas from him but the little one holds his arms tight around his grandfather's neck, hiding his face in his shoulder, '*non!*'

'Cécile phoned me, Sébastien. For some reason she seems to think that Thomas is not safe here any longer,' Angéline explains.

'Not safe? So, he'll be safer in your flat in Paris? Where he won't see a soul?' The latter remark sounds sarcastic.

Sylvia tries to soothe the situation. 'Sébastien – '

'If my daughter has a problem with her son being here, she can talk to me about it,' Sébastien says and leaves the room with Thomas in his arms.

'Sébastien!' Angéline's incisive voice cuts through to the hall. 'Don't think you can *always* have things your way!'

'Angéline, please,' Sylvia insists. 'Thomas is his grandson … He is right. Cécile should've talked to him about it.'

Angéline looks at the woman she has always been on good footing with. 'Maybe she should have, but she called *me*!' Angéline begins to leave the house. 'I'd better go,' she says with an annoyed face. 'Angéline … ' Sylvia attempts to try and make her reconsider but a few seconds later she hears the kitchen door that is being shut just a tad too firmly.

Across the hall Sébastien emerges from his father's study, Thomas close by him. 'The coast is clear,' he tells the boy. Thomas looks up at him with a triumphant smile on his face.

'Cécile is adding another week to her stay in England,' Sylvia explains as she leaves the room. 'That was the reason.' She looks at him. 'I don't need to tell you, you'd better phone Cécile and explain. Otherwise – '

'I'll try.' He and Thomas follow her into the kitchen and then outside where the late afternoon is cooled by a sea breeze that wafts through the trees. Thomas is ahead of them and runs towards the stables. 'Cécile must have misgivings about letting Thomas stay here any longer,' Sylvia says.

'I'll talk to her,' Sébastien replies. 'If she doesn't hang up on me … *Zut*,' he sighs. 'Thomas loves being here. Why doesn't she want what is good for her son?'

'I don't think that has anything to do with it, Sébastien,' Sylvia says. 'And Thomas shouldn't always have his way.'

He agrees. 'But, do you think he'd be better off in a Paris flat?'

Sylvia glances at him sideways. '*Non.*' She smiles, and they walk over to the field where Thomas has now joined his great-grandfather, who is standing by the fence admiring the horses.

'Did François arrive home all right?' his stepmother enquires.

'Yeah, fine. Madeleine was there. She sends her love.'

'Madeleine? Shouldn't she have been in school?'

'Yes. But she must've learned about her parents' divorce. That brought her home,' Sébastien replies while watching his father approach with Thomas in his wake.

'Excellent horse, that one,' Pierre says proudly, alluding to the fine black stallion. 'We'll be seeing a lot more of him on the racing tracks.'

Sébastien cannot object to that statement, yet something else is on his mind. 'Papa, do you have a moment?' he wonders.

'*Bien sûr.*'

Pierre calls over to one of the stable lads before he follows Sébastien. 'Can you put Isabelle in her box, please! Her owner doesn't want her outside too long.'

While Sylvia enters her vegetable garden, with Thomas close behind her, the two men make their way back to the house.

Pierre opens the door to his study for them to enter. 'How's François settling back in?' he asks.

'Fine. I mean, he will have a hard time ahead, naturally. With the sale of the house and the divorce.'

'Sale of his house?' That news surprises Pierre. 'Why?'

'Louise wants half of everything.'

' … Greedy, insatiable … ' he swallows the rest of his sentence. 'So, what is it you wanted to talk about?'

'The detective you mentioned – '

'Ah yes, Jules Garnier. I must have his phone number here somewhere.' He looks over to Sébastien. 'Have you decided to enlist his help?'

Sébastien nods. 'The police seem to be keeping holiday hours.'

The time-worn address directory that Pierre currently examines is one of many items that moved from Les Jonquières to La Fontenelle after Sylvia inherited the property upon M. Lambert's death. It has been on his father's desk for as long as Sébastien can remember.

'Here it is.' He points out the name as Sébastien takes his phone to store the number. 'He must be your age, Papa. Is he still working?'

'He is as much a *retraité* as I am,' is Pierre's reply and he lowers himself down into the armchair. 'Last thing I heard was that he had successfully solved a fraud case. But that was three years ago.'

Sébastien is briefly in two minds. 'Maybe I should hire a younger person,' he says.

'Why?' his father questions. 'You haven't even phoned him yet.'

Sébastien pulls the office chair closer and sits down too. He lets his phone slide from one hand to the other, and then clicks through the photos he took earlier that day. 'Look, Papa, we saw that Morgan in Marseille.'

'In Marseille? Well, maybe he lives there. Although … ' Pierre reflects upon an earlier instance. 'When we spoke,' he makes a movement with his hand, 'this was before you came back. When we first spoke, he mentioned he had a property in Monaco – '

'Monaco?' Sébastien has the photos on his screen and hands his father the phone.

'Yes, that's him. In Marseille you said?' Pierre has another look at the photos. 'That other man … I've a feeling I know him from somewhere.'

'You do?'

Pierre returns the phone to Sébastien. 'But I'm not sure. Maybe I met him at the races. Who's to say. I meet so many people.'

A quiet drizzle is falling down on the court as Sébastien opens the door of his car. He is about to get in when his grandson comes running towards him. 'Grandpapa! Can I come?'

Sébastien shakes his head. 'Not this time, Thomas. I'm going to town.'

'Can I come?'

'No, Thomas. I have some business.' He strokes the boy's head; his hair is now damp from the rain. 'You go and play. Or maybe you can help in the stables, *hein*?' He gets in and starts the engine while Thomas turns and runs back to the house.

After a few hundred metres, Sébastien leaves the forested area and he switches his windscreen-wipers on. When he turns off in the direction of Nice, the raindrops become more intense as the drizzle transforms into a harsh summer shower. Soon the road ahead is a shield of water, but as Sébastien reaches the city, the rain quickly diminishes and stops as he crosses its boundaries. Nice lies bathing in sunshine once more.

By a lucky coincidence, Jules Garnier is staying with his younger sister in the St. Augustin district, and

Sébastien makes his way to the street indicated by the detective. He looks up towards the block of flats and parks his car in its vicinity. Off the main roads, this street evokes a quiet respite from the usual city noises, with palm trees rustling gently in the breeze. He walks to the block of flats, and he has barely rung the bell when a voice sounds through the intercom, and the door is released. Sébastien enters the hall and goes to the elevator, following the directions he heard over the intercom moments before. On the top floor, he gets out and notices the man he has come to see standing in the doorway of one of the flats. His dark grey hair is neatly combed back, and in contrast, he wears a pair of track pants as if he just came back from a jog around the small park. His top is no more than a vest where some grey chest hair peeks from underneath.

'Monsieur Maréchal?' Jules Garnier offers him his hand. 'Bonjour. Come in.'

Sébastien enters the small and pleasant living-room of the flat and sits down in the chair Jules Garnier has pointed out. The latter glances at him and determines he looks like his father, Pierre, who he has known for so long now. 'Can I get you something?'

'Coffee? But there's no need to go through the extra trouble.'

'No trouble, I wouldn't mind a cup myself,' and Jules proceeds towards the kitchen, which is adjacent to the living-room. 'So, you've lived in Paris all these years, uh?' Jules asks from the kitchen among sounds of running water from the tap. 'I don't recall ever meeting you before, but as you're Pierre's boy, I'm sure we can come to some deal.'

Sébastien glances around the room where, apart from the table and a few chairs, a three-seater couch, with insignificant decorative motifs, is standing in front of a small TV screen. The wide prospect through the window attracts his attention and he rises from his chair. The view over the city is quite impressive.

Behind him he hears Jules enter the room and he turns to see him carry two mugs of coffee that he places on the table.

'Beautiful view you have here,' Sébastien says.

'Yes, it is. Better than what I have in Marseille, I can assure you.' He sits down. 'That's why I like it here.'

Sébastien sits down across from the man. He takes a few sugar lumps from the small bowl and stirs them through his coffee.

'How is Pierre?' Jules asks him. 'I haven't seen him for some time. But then, he's not often in Marseille, I gather.'

'Papa is OK. He had a bit of a heart scare about two weeks ago, but he's better now. On medication.'

Jules shakes his head. 'Your father should start taking things easy,' he says. 'He's always busy with his horses. Does he ever take the time for anything else?'

'Now that you mention it, I don't think I've ever seen him do anything else,' Sébastien replies. 'The horses are in his blood, that's what he lives for.'

'Yeah, I know the type,' Jules allows. 'Now, did you bring the information?'

Sébastien reaches for the large envelope he has brought. 'I've prints of the photos and here's a copy of the phone number. The police claim the car,' and he hands Jules the relevant photo, 'was stolen. And they claim the phone that was used was in the car, and therefore also stolen. Used by the criminals to draw attention away from themselves.'

Jules examines the pictures closely. His eyes rest longest on the photos Sébastien took in Marseille.

Quietness sets in as the latter keeps an inquisitive eye on the man sitting opposite. Eventually, Jules responds. 'I know who he is,' he tells Sébastien. 'This man, Morgan, or Gilbert Morgan as he's called, is someone who doesn't always take the legal path.'

'He told Papa he owns property in Monaco.'

Jules looks up at Sébastien. 'Is that his latest assertion? He wishes. *Non*, monsieur ... can I call you Sébastien?'

'Of course.'

'Sébastien, this man has hardly owned anything in his life. Legally. He's a British developer trying to make big money on the backs of others. He's quite ruthless, and gathers ruthless people around him.' Jules points to the other man in the photo. 'That's why it is so interesting that he is sitting there, being very chummy with this man.'

'Who's he then?'

'The head of police, Marseille Department. And I believe there was talk of him being transferred to Nice, as the head of police here is retiring.'

Sébastien takes the photo from him and looks at it as if the picture could somehow give him clarity. A puzzling look appears in his face when his thoughts are interrupted by Jules remark: 'Therefore, it would be interesting to find out why the police are stalling, to find the arsonist. I mean, forest fires in this area are normally given high priority, so why don't the police get on with it, *hein*?'

Sébastien draws his eyes away from the photo and looks at Jules. 'They don't seem to want to know there is an arsonist.'

Jules pulls a questioning face.

'They don't really believe that the fires were lit by ... by anyone other than ourselves.' Jules looks even more incredulous. 'Which is nonsense of course,' Sébastien goes on, 'because there are at least five witnesses, in both cases, who can testify to the opposite.'

Jules's face relaxes to its former expression. 'Right then ... ' A key turns in the door and a moment later a lady in her mid-sixties, carrying a bag with groceries, enters the room.

'Oh, meet my sister, Mathilde. One of Pierre Maréchal's boys, Sébastien,' Jules discloses to his sister.

'Madame,' Sébastien greets her.

'*Bonjour*, monsieur.' She makes her way into the kitchen where she lays out the groceries on the counter and opens a cupboard. 'Does M. Maréchal want anything?' she asks.

'No, Mathilde, thanks. We just had coffee.'

'But I brought some nice cakes from the patisserie!' She appears in the doorway. 'Are you sure?'

Sébastien is about to decline when Jules accepts. 'You don't want to refuse cakes from the patisserie, Sébastien,' he smiles. He stands up to make them all another coffee.

Sébastien gathers the information he has brought with him, and looks at the items and photos one by one, to see if there is anything that could give him more clarity, but he realises that only continuing investigation can solve that. Another cup of coffee appears before him, accompanied by an inviting looking piece of cake.

Jules takes Sébastien's information and puts it aside. 'You don't mind if I keep this, do you?'

'No. Please, and if there's anything you need to know, just call me.'

'I certainly will,' Jules replies.

After Sébastien has left and his sister is busy cooking that evening's dinner, Jules withdraws to the spare room and logs onto the internet on his notebook. He sends a somewhat encoded email to someone he knows inside the Marseille police force and asks for a meeting upon his return to the town.

When the Maréchal boy was here, he didn't want to let him know that he had dealt with Morgan before, regarding a case he worked on a few years ago. He had no idea that Gilbert Morgan had returned to France to continue his illegal activities. In the earlier case, Morgan had somehow slipped through the net and apparently laid low to then disappear into oblivion. It had annoyed him that he hadn't been able to nail the criminal.

He didn't want to reveal his surprise when he saw Morgan's face in the photos Sébastien Maréchal showed him this afternoon. He hopes that his man in Marseille -an informant with the police, and an old and trusted hand he has known for years- can provide him with more information. Trying to find some logic in the case Sébastien Maréchal presented to him, he reverts to his old habit of coding and documenting. When he came to spend vacation time in Nice, he wasn't prepared, but he now finds he needs hard-copy material. He never liked relying solely on digital forms of the evidence that he collected.

'Jules!' his sister calls from the other room. His door opens a few seconds later. 'Your phone is ringing,' she says, handing him the small device with its slow tune.

'Thanks.' He sees the name on the display and answers his phone. 'Well, that was quick. I only just sent you a message.'

'*Jules, I'm in Nice. We can meet tomorrow if that suits you,*' the man on the other end replies.

'Fine. Here? There's this little café inside the airport – '

'*Better somewhere less obvious, Jules,*' the man

interrupts. '*Uhm, do you know that little park not far from the stadium? There's a small local café …* ' Jules takes down the name of the establishment. 'Yes, That's fine. Nine o'clock – '

'*Please, Jules. I'm on holiday. Ten OK?*'

With the agreed time negotiated Jules puts his phone down. He hesitates for a moment and then searches for a number in his phone book. After listening for a while to the ringing of an unanswered call, Jules hears some noise on the other end and someone grumbles into the phone.

'Marcello?'

'*Si …* '

'Jules here. Jules Garnier. Are you busy?' There is more noise and the sound of crumpling paper.

'*Jules! It's been a while. Have you retired?*'

'Almost,' is Jules's reply. 'Are you still in the business?'

'*Whenever I'm needed. Something I can do for you?*'

'I need a numberplate checked.' Jules grabs the sheet of paper on which Sébastien has jotted down the details. 'Do you have a pen?' More noise and shuffling rings through in the mobile device; it has Jules wondering if he has interrupted something of importance.

'*OK.*' Marcello seems to have acquired something to write with and Jules gives him the numberplate details. 'Thanks, Marcello, appreciate it. I'll see if there's anything in it for you.'

'*Merci mon copain. You'll be hearing from me.*'

Jules puts his phone into the pocket of his track pants and opens the door of his room, where whiffs of pleasing aromas emanate from the kitchen into the hallway.

The following morning at Les Jonquières, the sun radiates her mid-morning rays into the kitchen where

Sébastien is inspecting his latest gadget, the newly installed water-purifier by the water tap next to the sink. He is pleased with the result and sips some of the transparent liquid.

Nicolas, who has just entered, looks at the situation but he refrains from voicing his opinion. He gazes at Sébastien who is enjoying his watery drink. '*Bien*,' the latter then says. 'Let's welcome the first customers.'

They walk outside into the yard and continue towards the first stable block where a horse trailer, pulled by a truck, obstructs the passage. The owner and an assistant get out of the truck and start to unhook the trailer door, and lower the ramp. The two horses inside the trailer smell the outside air and start shuffling their hooves in the wood shavings.

A woman in jeans and wearing a light chequered blouse approaches him. Her copper-coloured hair is held together with an indistinct elastic band. 'Monsieur Maréchal?'

Sébastien moves forward and greets her. 'Morning, madame LeGrand. So, these are your horses?'

'Yes,' she replies. 'Lucinda,' she points to the chestnut mare to the left, 'not her actual name but I preferred it when I got her. She won some races, when we were lucky, or she came in third or even lower. Then we tried her in show jumping. Not a success. She hated it. So, she's twelve now. We're thinking of using her as a breeding mare but, as I explained over the phone, we need the space.'

Sébastien watches the assistant untie the horse, and he reaches out to lend a hand with the bar. Slowly and with soothing words, the mare is backed out of the trailer. She's still nervous on her feet. Nicolas approaches and attaches a short lead line to the horse's head collar.

'She hates riding in the back of trailers,' Mme. LeGrand explains. 'One of our major worries when we took her to races.'

Sébastien strokes the animal on her neck to calm her.

'And here we have Arthur,' the horse owner says, referring to the dark brown stallion. 'He has a different name as well, but I don't understand the name-giving by horse breeders, they don't make sense. He's twenty and has finished racing.'

The stallion is less agitated and possibly more attuned to the routine of backing out of horse trailers. They don't have any problems unloading him.

'Shall we put them inside first, and see how they like their new surroundings?' Sébastien suggests.

The horses' owner takes Arthur by his halter, and Nicolas proceeds with the mare as they walk into the stable block. To the horses, the fresh straw in the spacious boxes is a pleasant change from the confinement of the horse trailer, and they readily settle in. The top half of the stable doors are left open for the horses to sniff the outside air and Mme. LeGrand follows Sébastien back to the house.

'Sorry, but my office isn't finished yet,' Sébastien says, opening the kitchen door so she can enter. He invites her to be seated on one of the chairs in the kitchen. 'Can I offer you something?'

'Glass of water if it's no trouble.'

Sébastien gives her a few forms to read through and fills a glass with water. 'Just some formalities,' he says as he puts the glass in front of her.

With quick glances, Mme. LeGrand scans the sheets of paper. 'It looks fine. Price is as we agreed,' she concludes and signs at the bottom. In her swift and efficient manner, the business is completed in a matter of minutes. 'When I have the time, I will come and ride my horses,' she says.

Sébastien stalls for a moment and then proposes the issue. 'Would you have a problem with other people riding them?'

For a moment the woman looks at him with questioning eyes. 'Others? I never thought about that.'

'I've had this idea, that maybe I can give riding lessons to children from the village,' Sébastien explains. 'There isn't much in that respect in this area.'

Mme. LeGrand stands up. 'Monsieur Maréchal – '

'Sébastien,' he says.

'Oh. Well. You can call me Lucille. Sébastien, I'm not sure if my horses are suitable for children to ride. They're used to racing, and they can be fiery animals if they feel like it.'

'But they're not *young* horses,' he reasons.

Lucille has presented herself as a woman who doesn't like to mince her words, Sébastien finds, and her bearing is that of a person carrying out deeds in a decisive manner, but she now seems unsure. 'Whatever money is earned with riding lessons, I could deduct from the stabling fees,' he adds.

'Money is not the issue here. It's the fact that these horses have hardly been ridden by children! What if something happens?'

'There might be adults, too, interested in riding,' Sébastien argues.

Lucille is not convinced. 'Let's leave it for now.' She walks to the door. 'I have some more business to attend to. Bonjour,' she says and shakes his hand. She swiftly makes her way out into the yard where her assistant has turned the truck around and she gets in. With a wave of her hand through the open window, they drive off on the unpaved road. Sébastien watches the back of the horse trailer as it quickly disappears from sight and he then makes his way to the stables. Lucinda and Arthur seem satisfied in their new home, and Sébastien continues to check on the stable block at the far end of the yard. It is here where he finds Nicolas, Raymond and Julien. Inside, they are busy preparing the new boxes for horses that will be housed here. Since the rebuild and other jobs completed, they are the only men left working at Les Jonquières.

7

Sylvia looks up from her work in the flower garden when a small yellow car drives up in front of the house. It disappears momentarily from her view, but then whisks around and stops. A young, spirited woman jumps out. Her short dark hair shows in peaky strands from under a bright bandanna that she has tied around her head. 'Mamie!' She waves as she sees her grandmother in the garden, who starts walking towards her. 'Cécile!'

They embrace the moment they reach each other. 'Cécile. How are you? I wasn't expecting you back?'

'Well, I'm here now,' Cécile replies. She casts her eyes around the grounds. 'Where is Thomas?'

'Oh, don't worry about him,' Sylvia says. 'He's having a grand old time. He and your father have become quite good friends, you know.'

The young woman's face changes to a blank expression. Sylvia puts her arm around Cécile's waist. 'Don't get mad about it. Where's the harm in Thomas getting to know his grandfather. But, I thought you wanted to extend your stay in England? How come you've changed your mind?'

'Something worried me so I decided to come home sooner,' her granddaughter says.

Sylvia leads Cécile into the coolness of the kitchen.

'They're at Les Jonquières,' she explains. 'Sébastien has worked very hard, with the help of some men from the village and the contractor he has hired.' She pours Cécile some iced tea while the latter is pacing up and down the tiled kitchen floor. 'There you are, darling,' Sylvia offers, and places the ice-tea on the table. 'Your papa has some horses in his stables already!'

'Grand-mère.' Cécile's voice sounds concerned. 'He hasn't let Thomas on any of those horses, has he?'

'You know your father knows how you feel about that,' Sylvia expresses.

Cécile stops to face her grandmother. 'Mamie, that's not what I asked! Has he put Thomas on any of these animals?'

Sylvia nods. 'Once. I saw them once when he took Thomas with him in the saddle.'

Cécile shakes her head and sighs in disbelieve. 'How could you? How could you allow it?!'

'It was totally harmless, Cécile. And Thomas loved it!'

Cécile recalls a similar instance when she was barely four years old, on a horse in front of her father. She had screamed until her mother had taken her from the saddle, leaving her father rather displeased. She looks at Sylvia with an angry expression. 'I can't imagine Thomas enjoying a ride on those animals.'

Sylvia comes towards her and places a hand against her granddaughter's cheek. 'Cécile, he's been in the saddle with me, too. There's no harm. Please, don't get upset.'

Cécile's attitude towards her grandmother changes and the look on her face disturbs Sylvia. 'Please Cécile. Thomas is different. It seems ... he has no fear.'

The young woman moves away from Sylvia. 'Having no fear killed my mother,' she says. 'I'm going over there.'

'Cécile, please, be reasonable. You were only four. How could you have known what your mother felt when she made that jump?'

Cécile looks at her grandmother, then walks out the

door. Within a minute Sylvia hears her speeding off the forecourt, making her way towards Les Jonquières. As a mother, Sylvia can relate to the worry Cécile feels. She herself was always fearful when her son François was on one of his adventurous sojourns, either with his older brother Sébastien, or when he went off on his own, leaving her agonising about what might happen.

Cécile presses her foot down hard on the accelerator until her small car goes above the local speed limit. Since she left the area, she hasn't driven in this direction often but she has no problem finding the way along the narrow country lane. She almost hits a boulder by the road when speeding through this area too fast. Reluctantly, she brakes but picks up speed again as soon as she is on a straight stretch. It doesn't take her long to reach Les Jonquières, and she speeds up the unpaved road that leads to the house and the adjacent stables. She casts a glance to her right where a couple of horses graze in the pasture. A moment later, she sees a few men walking across the yard, and she stops her car.

'Excuse me,' she says as she gets out. 'My father, Sébastien Maréchal. Where can I find him?'

Nicolas points towards a small *carrière* behind a fence. '*Là-bas*, in the lunging ring.' Nicolas watches her with some curiosity as Cécile goes towards the training track he indicated.

From behind a few bushes, the sand circle comes into her view, and her face softens when she sees her father holding a lunge line with a pony attached to the other end, clearly enjoying what he always enjoyed the most. The feeling of seeing her father after the years that have passed instantly turns to shock when she sees it is her small son sitting on the back of that pony. All at once she dives underneath the fencing and rushes towards the horse. Sébastien looks on in disbelief as he sees his daughter appear from out of nowhere. Before he can utter a word, his grandson is snatched from the saddle, and his daughter's face shows a fit of anger he has never experienced in her.

'How *could* you! *Nothing* is safe in your hands!' she says in a biting tone. With her son in her arms, she hurries to leave the unsafe space.

'Maman,' Thomas whimpers, as he is aware of his mother's actions that indicate that she forbids him to ride his pony. Cécile is halfway to her car when her father realises what happened within these few seconds. 'Cécile!' He makes his way out of the ring and runs after her. 'Cécile!'

His daughter is already behind the wheel of her car with Thomas crying next to her. Tears, caused by the shock of his mother's sudden outburst.

'Cécile!' Sébastien tries to open the car door, but his daughter turns around and speeds off, leaving her father behind, bewildered and hurt. He sees dust whirling up from the dirt road, and small stones scattering from under the tyres. 'Careful!' but his words of warning and concern are lost. He drops his shoulders in defeat. Nicolas looks at him. Judging by what he has been told about the daughter, he is aware that this blunt rejection by the young woman is not helping Sébastien Maréchal.

Thomas is still crying when his mother pulls up in the court of La Fontenelle. 'Thomas, please,' Cécile says, 'and take off that silly hat.' She undoes the strap of the riding helmet and lifts Thomas from the car, chucking the helmet out of sight. 'You can stop crying now,' she says, but the tears keep rolling down her son's face. She takes him by the hand and walks into the house, where her grandmother has not moved from the kitchen. Thomas lets go of his mother's hand, and with a defeated attitude, walks over to his great-grandmother who shows more sympathy. The latter sits down and lifts Thomas onto her lap.

'I don't know why he keeps crying,' Cécile says. 'Are his things upstairs?' Without waiting for an answer, she goes into the hall, and soon after Sylvia hears her in the room above their head.

'Thomas,' she soothes, 'Maman has come to take you home.'

Sylvia strokes the boy's hair and face as Thomas leans his head against his great-grandmother's bosom, and gradually the sobbing subsides.

'You knew you were only here for a short while,' Sylvia says. 'Now it's time to go home again.'

'I don't want to,' Thomas's muffled voice sounds.

'You can always come for a visit.'

'Maman will be angry again.'

Sylvia looks at the boy's face. 'Was she angry?'

Thomas nods. 'I was riding my pony.'

'But with Grand-père, *non*?'

'*Oui*. But Maman doesn't like horses, and she pulled me from my pony.'

Sylvia's face shows disbelief. 'She pulled you from your pony?'

Cécile overhears the last words as she enters. 'Yes, I did,' she says matter-of-factly. 'So often I have raised my concern about Thomas riding horses. Do you now understand that worry drove me back sooner than planned?' She looks at her grandmother in a somewhat accusatory manner. 'Say goodbye now, Thomas. We're leaving.'

She lifts her son from Sylvia's lap and is about to

walk to the door when it opens and Pierre enters. 'Cécile! Why didn't you say you were coming?' His initial surprise only lasts a few seconds before it makes way for a questioning look when he sees the subdued faces turning his way. 'What's going on?'

'I'm back and I've come to take Thomas home,' Cécile merely states.

'So, you were going to run out without even saying hello, or goodbye,' Pierre says. He looks at his granddaughter, desiring an explanation.

' … Well. Goodbye Grand-père.' She reaches out to kiss him on his cheek, but Pierre is not deceived. He grabs her elbow. 'The way I understood it, you extended your stay in England, and now all of a sudden you're here? And why has Thomas been crying?' He strokes the head of the boy whose face shows signs of the tears he has shed. 'Was he so happy to see you?'

Sylvia finds that remark somewhat harsh. 'Pierre, please.'

The respect Cécile feels for her grandfather prevents her from going against the elderly man's authority.

'I was worried,' she says. 'Worried that my son was going to be put on those horses … You see, Angéline was a bit … vague. She couldn't really say why she had not taken Thomas back with her. So, I put two and two together and – '

'And you decided to spoil the fun your son was having and take him back to that city!'

Sylvia approaches and puts a hand on her husband's arm. 'Pierre. Please. She is his mother.'

Pierre ignores his wife. 'Why Cécile? Why? Just because you hate horses, doesn't mean your son should feel the same about the animals!'

'Grand-père!' Cécile calls out in desperation. 'I …

You know what I went through after Maman died and still … you accuse me … ' Cécile hides her face in her hands. Her grandmother puts an arm around her shoulder. 'Enough now,' she tells Pierre. 'Outside you.'

Pierre sighs and turns to walk to the door. 'Take Thomas with you,' his wife says.

When the two have left the room, Sylvia sits Cécile down and hands her some tissues.

'It's only natural that you worry about your child, Cécile,' she says after a while. 'But, I can't say I agree with your reasoning.'

Cécile's looks up at her with a tearful face.

'Thomas is only a young boy, but he just loves being around the horses. Around any animal,' her grandmother goes on. 'There's this big white dog, too – '

'A big white dog?'

'Yes, he belongs to a man in the village, and sometimes the dog wanders over here, and Thomas loves to play with him.'

'He's not dangerous, is he?'

'Cécile,' Sylvia soothes. 'The dog is harmless! Actually, it was the dog that found your uncle in the woods. After dark, when everyone else had given up the search, the dog stayed and found François.'

Cécile wipes her face and looks at her grandmother. Sylvia gives her a meaningful look. 'So you see, I'm not at all worried when the dog chooses to play with Thomas.'

'Yes, but it's the horses, Mamie. I … I just can't allow my son to ride them.' She starts fidgeting with her tissue. 'I just … It reminds me too much of … how my mother was killed.' She looks at Sylvia. 'You do understand?'

'It was a freak accident, Cécile.'

'Maybe, but I can't … I won't allow Thomas to ride

● ● ●

135

them.' Her last words sound decisive. 'So, I hope you're not angry about my decision.' She wipes a last tear from her cheek and blows her nose. 'Let's see where they've gone. We really should go now,' she says as she stands up.

'But Cécile! Why don't you just stay for a few more days?'

Cécile looks at her grandmother and knows too well the intention behind her offer. 'No, not now, Mamie. I should get back to work as well. They actually only gave me ten days, to attend the conference. As it had to do with work.'

Sylvia looks out of the window when she hears some horses being led back to their stables. 'But, you've hardly spoken to your father,' she then says. 'Don't you think this is a good time for you to … to draw a bit closer to your papa?'

'Mamie … ' Cécile doesn't feel the need to discuss the subject, and she opens the door to walk out.

The regret that Sylvia feels is not only for this latest attempt to have her granddaughter talk to her father. She refrains from following Cécile outside.

Nicolas has persuaded Sébastien to come and try the new vintage that has been delivered to Michél's establishment.

The only advice Nicolas can give Sébastien in his troubled state is distraction. Michél stands by their table, curious to know what they think of the wine, but Sébastien has no desire to rave about the drink, while Nicolas nods approvingly to Michél.

'I have three daughters,' he then says. 'But my situation can't be compared to yours.'

'Why not?' Sebastien asks.

'I was always home.' He looks at him sideways. 'Of

course we had our differences, like in any family, but we always got along.'

'Mm,' is Sébastien's reply and with a certain disregard, he gulps the wine down.

'If you don't mind me saying,' Nicolas offers, 'I do think that your daughter overreacted.'

Sébastien looks at him with assent in his eyes.

'If she was one of mine, I'd have told her off,' Nicolas says.

Sébastien realises that that is an authority he lost long ago when he let his parents raise his little girl. 'Yes, but she never gave me a chance. She was gone in no time. You saw for yourself.' He takes the bottle and refills their glasses. Michél places some cheese in front of them to have with the wine, but it doesn't entice Sébastien. His thoughts are elsewhere. He is indecisive about what to do, about what action he should take. His daughter has made him feel like a child, who has done great wrong and needs to be punished for his awful deed.

His feelings of anger replaced his feelings of sadness because of her treatment of him.

And Thomas, it still hurts his heart when he thinks of how the boy was crying, and him not having been able to console his grandson. Had she really become so selfish? Could she only think about her own feelings? He found it hard to believe that his parents had instilled such insolence in the woman who was his daughter. As the parent who has failed his child in the past, he feels it is up to him to try and reach her, but reconciliation with his daughter seems further away than ever.

The following morning Sébastien walks the long stretch to the beach on foot. He strolls along the sandy bridleway, in thought and his eyes cast down. Through the foliage overhead, patches of blue sky interact with the green of the canopies. Unseen birds sing on branches and in the distance a hare shoots over the path. The June heat is kept at bay by the trees and bushes that only allow dappled sunlight to filter through. His feet shuffle over the sand through the shady patches as he finds his way to the beach. The brightness that meets him there blinds him for an instant, but he continues to walk along, there where shrubs border the beach. After a while and with a heavy sigh, he sits down on a rock bathed in the bright light of the sun but it doesn't disturb him. The sleepless night has left his head numb, and the recollection of yesterday's abrupt interference of the harmless riding lesson he was giving his grandson, still bothers him. He squints his eyes when he looks across the sea and listens to the surf rippling onto the beach. The calming sound prompts him to get up and walk to the tranquillity of the lapping water, where he continues to stroll along in the wet sand. At times his feet are washed over by the seawater, leaving his trainers and jeans wet, but that too does not bother him. When he reaches the other end of the beach, he hesitates but decides against walking to Les Jonquières. He turns around and begins the long walk back. Halfway down the beach, he hears the dull sound of hooves clattering on the sand. The sound is so common to him that he keeps walking. The horse passes him and its rider's copper-coloured hair waves in the breeze. The woman turns her horse around and approaches him.

'Monsieur Maréchal!'

She stops in front of him. 'Sébastien. Going on foot? Quite unusual.'

Sébastien looks up at her smiling face, not in the mood for conversation. 'It can have its advantages,' he says.

Lucille casts him a questioning glance.

'Nicely relaxing.'

She shows a quick smile. 'Oh, I've thought about what you said. About those riding lessons.' Her horse throws his head back, eager to move on. 'I suppose it's not a bad idea. We can discuss it.'

Sébastien nods. 'Fine. Call me.' He moves on as Lucille pulls the rein, and her horse speeds off in the opposite direction. He sees her galloping to the far end while he makes his way to the edge of the beach where the rocks and shrubs border the sand. He climbs over some rocks and finds his way back to the bridle path. Behind him, he hears Lucille galloping along the beach until she is out of earshot. He is in no rush to get back to La Fontenelle, and he calmly strolls through the pine trees, along the sandy path to his parents' house.

Entering the yard, he witnesses some jockeys riding towards the *parcour* for their training. His father follows them as he walks beside the trainer, busy in conversation. He sees his stepmother go into the stables, no doubt to saddle up her horse and go for a ride. Everything emits such a tranquil, everyday atmosphere it almost annoys Sébastien to see it. He goes into the house and walks through the hall and up the stairs to his room. In the room, he waits somewhat indecisively by the door, then walks over to the window, and sits down in the chair that overlooks the forecourt. The sky is stark blue, and the sun beats down on the terrace. There is hardly any life in the fields beyond, and birds seem to have ceased their song. He doesn't pay attention to the ringing of his phone that he left on a shelf by his bed. After a few moments, it stops, and he becomes absorbed in thought once more.

When he finally gets up from his chair and picks up his phone, he notices that it was Jules Garnier who tried to call him. Several times. To Sébastien, however, the importance of the situation with the arson attacks has faded into the background. Still, as he walks down the stairs, he returns the call. He accepts Jules's request for a meeting and makes a note, for he is not in the mood to go there today.

A few days later, Sébastien parks his car not far from a café near the stadium in Nice at Jules Garnier's suggestion. He finds him at the back of the establishment, talking to someone Sébastien hasn't seen before. The greying man says goodbye when Sébastien approaches.

'An old friend,' Jules explains. 'Sit down, *s'il te plaît.*'

Sébastien pulls up a chair and sits down while Jules takes out a few sheets of paper. In the margins of the printed matter, some hand-scribbled annotations are visible. 'The man who just left would like it if you don't remember you ever saw him,' Jules says. 'He's my informant.'

'Your whistle blower,' Sébastien rectifies. Jules just looks at him and shakes his head. 'Just forget you ever saw him. Now, here is what I've discovered so far,' handing Sebastien the sheets of paper. 'Turns out that the man in the photo you took in Marseille is indeed a superior at the Marseille Police Department, but not the head of police any more. My contact has found proof that he has dealings with Morgan.' Sébastien looks at him with anticipation. 'But, I can't supply that proof yet,' Jules continues.

'Why not?'

'I must have more information,' Jules says. 'Anyway,' he then goes on, 'that's not why you hired me. You want to know who caused the arson attacks on your property.'

A waiter interrupts their conversation and puts two cups of coffee down on their table. '*Merci.*' Jules waits for the man to disappear. 'The car that was seen, *was* stolen. It belongs to someone from Montpellier. Also the mobile phone. That person has since been reunited with his possessions and didn't have anything to do with the fires on your property.'

'OK. But, what is the connection with Morgan in this?'

'Morgan develops property. He needs land and when he can't get it legally, he will use intimidation to get it. So, he hired someone to set fire to your property. And that person felt that the way to deal with it, was to use a stolen car.'

'And where is that man? Do you know who he is? Have the police found him already?'

Jules slowly stirs his coffee. 'The police are a bit sluggish but that's because they are busy with the whole picture. They want to go to the top and then make the arrests.'

Sébastien is briefly in two minds. 'Couldn't you have told me this over the phone?' he then says. 'I could've come up with such theories myself.' He gets up to leave but Jules pulls his sleeve and indicates for him to sit down again.

'What's with you?' Jules sounds annoyed but surprised at the same time. 'Morgan deals with black market money and wants to whitewash it. He and that man he's so chummy with in your photograph, go back a long way. I'm interested in finding out to what extent that police officer is involved in Morgan's schemes.' He looks Sébastien straight in his eyes. 'And I could use your help.'

Sébastien is not enthusiastic about that idea.

'What if you just *pretend* that you want to sell,' Jules continues. 'We wait until the deal is done, *et voilá*, we've got him!'

Sébastien shakes his head. 'Les Jonquières is not for sale,' he merely says.

'You won't really sell it. We just get him to that point and then,' Jules slaps his hands together, 'the police move in and make the arrest!'

'I don't want to get involved,' Sébastien says.

The man's face opposite him changes to discontent.

'I'm sorry, but no.' Sébastien stands up. 'I'm sure you can think of something else to catch Morgan in the act.'

Jules looks up at him. 'No, Sébastien. I won't.'

Sébastien throws a few Euro coins on the table to pay for the coffee he never ordered, but Jules shoves it back his way. 'No need.'

While Jules lets him know he'll be in touch, Sébastien leaves the café, disappointed with the results Jules has come up with. The man who caused the fires has not been caught, and he doubts whether Jules knows who the culprit is. Everything is very dubious, and it could mean that something else could happen at Les Jonquières. He walks across to his car and is about to get in when he sees a familiar face approaching on the pavement. To stay inconspicuous, Sébastien quickly gets into his car. From behind the windscreen, he observes Morgan as he passes and walks onward. He watches the man who is the cause of his troubles walk to the end of the street and then cross. Sébastien looks at the café he just came out of and pauses for a moment, but as he is about to get out of his car, he sees Jules leaving the establishment and walking in the opposite direction. Sébastien starts the engine and quickly turns. He drives his car alongside the pavement and briefly honks to catch Jules's attention. Jules looks at him with some surprise. 'Get in, Jules,' Sébastien urges him through the open window. Jules doesn't think twice and grabs the door handle. 'Do you want to give me a ride?'

Sébastien turns the car around in a hurry. 'I just saw Morgan go down this street.'

'Morgan? Are you sure?'

Sébastien gathers speed, and soon they spot the man strolling along. He doesn't seem to be in a hurry.

'What is he doing in Nice?' Jules wonders. Sébastien shrugs his shoulders and watches as the man meanders along as if he were a tourist taking in the sights. 'Have you actually found out where he lives?' he asks Jules.

'In Marseille,' is the reply. 'In a dodgy neighbourhood. But I suppose, for him that's the best area to find like-minded comrades.'

Their eyes keenly follow the movements of the man, Morgan, who presently stops for a traffic light. He waits patiently and crosses when the light jumps to green. Amid other pedestrians, he ambles along. Once he has crossed the street, he walks towards a bench in a small park and sits down. It doesn't take long before someone joins him. Sébastien is obliged to drive his car out of the way of other traffic and he stops by the side of the road.

'What the … ' Jules utters. Almost simultaneously their faces turn to surprise when they see it is Jules's informer who has just joined Morgan on the bench.

'Did you know about this?' Sébastien asks.

Jules shakes his head. 'This is getting more and more interesting,' he replies. 'Morgan has found his like-minded comrades … among police officers.'

Sébastien has taken out his telephone. He zooms in and swiftly takes a few photos.

'Send me those too, will you,' Jules says.

'A shame we can't hear what they're discussing,'

Sébastien says.

Jules agrees. 'It could be a very interesting conversation.'

They wait in the car for the men to each go their own way. Sébastien is about to pull away from the side of the road when Jules grabs the door handle and gets out. It takes Sébastien by surprise, and he watches as Jules walks hurriedly along the street and overtake his 'inside man'. What Sébastien can see from behind the wheel is that an amicable conversation ensues. '*Ce qui se passe là,*' he mutters under his breath. Even though he is curious to know what is going on, he remains in the car and waits for Jules to return. By then, the informer has boarded a bus and is gone. Sébastien looks at Jules as he steps back into the car and asks for an explanation.

'You won't believe this,' Jules says, 'but he actually nibbles on both sides. So to speak. He has befriended Morgan just to find out what he is up to. Morgan has been on the prowl inside the police force. Bloody nerve.'

'I get the impression he totally lacks respect for everything and everybody,' Sébastien says and shakes his head. He pulls away and accelerates. 'Can I drop you somewhere?'

'If it's no trouble. At my sister's. I think I need to contact a few people.'

It doesn't take long before Sébastien drops off Jules and then continues on his way to La Fontenelle.

When he leaves Nice behind, Sébastien feels irritated and none the wiser. The worry about another potential attack on his property festers at the back of his mind. He decides not to go to Fontenelle and drives a bit further down the road to enter the road that connects with the unpaved lane that will take him to Les Jonquières. His mind is eased by the natural surroundings on either side of the country lane. A few minutes later he sees the training track on the left with the forest beyond. To his right are the pastures, where now seven horses are grazing in the sun, or sheltering by trees that are scattered over the landscape. It occurs to him that no person in their right mind would want such a landscape to disappear.

Before him, his house looms up. Suddenly, his mind is triggered by an instant when he was a nine-year-old boy, and the first time he ever saw this. The day he arrived here, accompanied by César, who had come with him to ensure that the apple of his eye would find a good home with his newfound father. In the backseat he sat, with Belle beside him, gazing out at the unfamiliar landscape. Until then he was only used to the mountains of Alpes-Maritimes. At the time, it hadn't taken him long to discover that this man who trained horses and who was his father, was not a person he wanted to live with. He had pleaded with César to take them back to the familiarity of the farm, and the pastures in the mountains, but César had been unrelenting. He wasn't a young man any more, and he had felt that the chance for Sébastien to live with his biological father had come at the right time. Pierre Maréchal went through a difficult period after the sudden appearance of his son Sébastien. A son he never knew existed. It would not have taken much for Pierre to lose everything he had, caused by his misjudging the way his fiancée Sylvia would respond. She had broken off the engagement because he had concealed a former love interest and the existence of his son.

His father Pierre not only neglected him but was also in grave danger of losing Les Jonquières due to the gambling addiction he had developed. In that time of distress and helplessness, he had written to Célestine, the elderly lady who was keeping house for César. She arrived a few days later and brought much-needed cheer and happiness back into the sour atmosphere that had lingered in and around the house. Célestine's presence had given him courage, and all those years ago he had been adamant to bring his father and Sylvia back together. In the process, he had proven that he did like horses and, after he had nursed Monseigneur back to health, he had won a race. Sébastien now relives these accomplishments that he achieved at such a young age. At the age of nine!

He has reached the yard but suddenly he turns his car around and drives back the way he came, along the unpaved road and back onto the main road.

Two and a half hours later he finds himself in the vicinity of the Old Port in Marseille and he stops in a street across from a fitness centre. He observes the building with the required images on its windows of slim people in fitness gear, holding weights and other forms of exercise apparatus. The name of the club looks familiar to him. He was a member of the same fitness club in Paris for a while until he found that training inside an air-conditioned building was not his ambition. Gazing at the building, he tries to discover if there is any sign of his daughter, but he realises the best way to find her, is to go in. He locks his car and waits for a few cars to pass before crossing the road.

Inside, the coolness of the air hits him. He goes towards the reception desk, all the while looking around the space, spotting a small eatery to the left and a large room with fitness equipment behind a glass wall. It isn't busy there. The young woman behind the desk looks at him with a friendly face. 'What can I do for you, monsieur?'

'Uh … I'd like to see my daughter. Cécile Maréchal. I

believe she works here.'

The look the young lady gives him is a bit too thorough for his taste.

'She does work here, at this branch?' Sébastien questions.

'*Oui, oui.* You are correct.'

'And … Is she here? Is she working today?'

The young woman nods affirmatively, and her hand reaches for the telephone in front of her. 'I'll let her know you're here. Please take a seat. Over there,' she indicates.

Sébastien looks behind him and sees the seating area but he remains on his feet. He spots brochures with the weekly program on the desk and takes one. He notices his daughter's name next to some of the classes. Slowly, he backs away from the reception desk and strolls around the reception area. He peeks through the large glass wall where someone is putting all his strength into a weightlifting machine. He is dripping with sweat. Sébastien looks at another person in training, skipping a rope with such speed that the rotation of the rope is hardly visible to the naked eye.

'Monsieur.' The young woman behind the desk draws his attention. 'She's just finishing, she won't be long.'

'*Merci.*'

He lingers and then sits down but soon is on his feet again. He can't say if it's his impatience or the waiting that makes him feel nervous. After an amount of time has elapsed, he finally spots his daughter coming through a sliding door. She gives him a somewhat distant look. 'Papa,' she says matter-of-factly.

'Cécile. Cécile, can we go somewhere and talk?'

Cécile motions towards the small eatery. 'I'm on duty, I can't leave the building now.'

They walk towards a table and sit down across from

each other. 'How are you?' Sébastien asks. 'How's Thomas?'

'We're fine. Papa, what is it you want to talk about?'

Sébastien takes his time, then he looks at her. 'I wish we could get along better … That's what I wish, Cécile. So, that we can discuss things – '

'Discuss things.' Cécile's comment sounds sceptical.

'Yes, for instance, this situation with Thomas.'

'Papa, you've never shown any interest in my child, and now all of a sudden – '

'Because you kept a distance, Cécile. You've built a relationship with your stepmother, your ex-stepmother, but you hardly want to talk to me.'

'She's a friend, Papa.'

Sébastien must acknowledge that his daughter always got along well with Angéline. 'I am sorry, Cécile, that I haven't always been there for you. I realise the fault is mine – '

'It's no one's *fault*, Papa. After all this time, I've come to understand the situation you were in … when Maman … after she had her accident. It must have been horrible for you, too.'

They look at each other. 'But, I feel I've failed you,' Sébastien then says. 'You were so young.'

'Look, Papa, I'm glad you've come back to Les Jonquières. For that's where you belong. But Thomas and I do not belong there. So, please. Don't try to push your way of life onto others.'

'Cécile, that is not what I tried to do,' Sébastien says. 'It's Thomas. He was around the stables all the time – '

'That's one thing I don't want him to do,' Cécile says sharply. 'He is *my* son, and I don't want him to become familiar with things he can't have anyway. It will only make him miserable.'

'Fine, but why do you send him to stay with Sylvia and Pierre then? Thomas can hardly avoid horses there, can he?'

Cécile sighs. 'We will never agree on this subject, Papa.' She stands up. 'I have to get back to work.' Sébastien abruptly rises from his chair and grabs her by her arm. 'Cécile, please.' His daughter gives him a somewhat languid look.

He affectionately holds his hand against her cheek. 'Come for a visit every once in a while,' he says before Cécile turns and walks away. He watches her disappear through the sliding doors. Suddenly, he feels tired and he lowers himself onto the chair. For a while, he sits there, until a young man behind the counter asks him if he needs anything. Sébastien looks in the direction of the voice, then he stands up and walks over to the cold section where he takes out a bottle of water. After he has paid for the item, he goes outside and walks across to his car. When he drives away, his daughter's face is visible behind a window on the top floor of the fitness building.

8

*T*he sun is just spreading a few rays through the trees when Sylvia strolls along the garden path to sit down on a bench near the patio. With her cup of coffee in her hand, she enjoys the tranquillity of the early morning, when birds can be heard in the trees, and the horses still restfully linger in the fields around the house. Off in the distance, a dog barks. Dogs have always been absent from La Fontenelle, but here and there a cat ambles around the property. On this bright day, Sébastien leaves the house by the kitchen door and finds his stepmother outside where he joins her on the bench. 'Morning, Sébastien.'

'Beautiful day again,' Sébastien replies. Sylvia nods and looks at him. 'How is everything at Les Jonquières? I really should come and see what it looks like now.'

'Good. It is finished, ready to move back in, but it needs furniture. I've to ask Papa where he stored all my belongings. Strangely, that is one thing that hasn't been on my mind at all.'

'All your things are here. In the large shed,' Sylvia says.

'Are they?'

'Yes. Didn't you know?'

Sébastien shakes his head. 'My own doing, I suppose. I never asked what happened to my furniture.'

'I'll show you in a moment. Let me finish my coffee first,' Sylvia says.

While they enjoy the morning becoming brighter and the sun more intense, they see jockeys gradually emerging from their living quarters and making their way to fields and stables. Sylvia puts her empty cup down, and they rise from their comfortable spot. Meandering through horses that have been taken from the fields, they cross the yard and walk towards a large shed at the end of it. 'Do you have a key?' Sébastien asks.

'It's never locked,' Sylvia says. She opens the door, and a musty smell comes their way. 'Not much fresh air flows through here.'

Through streaks of daylight that find their way into this large space, they see dust particles and hazy air hover around objects covered with large pieces of faded fabric. 'Did I really have all that stuff at Jonquières?' Sébastien slowly walks towards the shapes under the cloth and then lifts the fabric. Dust and dirt fly about the shed. 'It'll take a moving van to move all that back to my house.'

Sylvia also lifts a piece of fabric, and more furniture becomes visible. After all these years in the modernity of his Paris apartment, the furniture he sees emerging from under the cloth appears somewhat unfashionable to him. 'It does look outdated,' Sébastien concludes, lifting another piece of fabric.

'Do you think so? We have the same style,' Sylvia says. 'It only needs cleaning, and then you'll see how nice it all looks.'

Sébastien is not so sure about that, and he wonders whether he should purchase new furniture. They drop the fabric back in its place and walk outside. The sun is bright in the blue sky when they pass the stable blocks. By this time Pierre has also made his way to the stables and is busy instructing jockeys and informing them about the next race.

'Morning, Papa,' Sébastien says as Sylvia kisses her husband.

'Morning. Say, Sébastien, you should come with us

this Sunday. There's a big race in Nice.'

Sébastien looks at the horses and their jockeys, ready for their training. '*D'accord*, I think I'll come.' He strokes one of the horses on his neck. 'It has been a long time since I was at a race.'

Sylvia and Pierre smile at him contentedly. 'Come,' Sylvia says and takes Sébastien by his arm. 'Let's ride to the beach.'

They make their way inside the stables while Pierre and his trainer follow the horses to the training track.

Sébastien decides to leave Jeune Homme in the pasture and saddles one of his father's horses as Sylvia attaches the girth on her own horse.

Outside in the sunny yard, they mount their horses and trot to the forest track. Sylvia spurs her horse into a gallop, and Sébastien doesn't lag behind. They race through the trees until they reach the green divide where the old Oak tree stands placidly. Long ago, the Oak was nicknamed Fairy Tree because of the many generations who courted beneath it.

It was here on the green, all those years ago when Sylvia first taught him to ride. His father, Pierre, hadn't kept his promise. Although he had insisted that Sébastien should learn to ride a horse if he was to live at Les Jonquières, it had been the lessons Sylvia had given him during their secret meetings that had made him familiar with the sport.

'*Allez, on y vas!*' Sylvia calls out, and they race onward to the beach. The shore comes into view, and the horses' hooves hit the sandy surface. They pull the reins to continue at a slower pace. There's a mild breeze and waves ripple onto the beach while a few seagulls utter their shrill cries above them.

'Has Cécile been in touch?' Sébastien asks at a given

moment.

Sylvia looks at him. 'She calls occasionally.'

'I went to see her,' Sébastien says.

His confession pleases Sylvia, but she is surprised at the same time. 'When was this?'

'Oh. Last week.' He dismounts and takes the rein in his hand. 'She was friendly.'

'Friendly.' Sylvia lets herself slide out of the saddle as well, and they stroll along on the water's edge. 'Well, at least that's something. Usually, when she calls, she doesn't even like your name mentioned.'

Sébastien picks up a smooth shell from the beach and looks at it.

'You know, Sébastien, I think that Cécile is just as sad about the troubled relationship you two have.'

'That's not the impression I got,' Sébastien says, and he blows the sand off his shell.

'Sébastien … ' Sylvia says in a soothing voice, but the former has spotted the white dog, emerging from the forest on the far end of the beach. 'Look,' Sébastien says. 'Métèque is on patrol again.'

Sylvia recognises her stepson's avoidance when it comes to discussing difficult issues. 'You should really try harder with her. She's a good girl, and a good mother.'

The last comment makes Sébastien turn his face her way. 'A good mother. A good mother who forbids her son the simple things in life.'

'Sébastien, you know she has her reasons. Don't make things harder than they already are.' Sylvia shakes her head. 'And don't look at things just from your own standpoint … Give it time.'

'*Oui, Maman.*'

Sylvia nudges him in his side and jumps back on her horse. 'Race you!'

Sebastien can't jump back into his saddle fast enough and speed after her. This is one race he doesn't want to lose. When he is alongside her, he raises his voice and suggests a ride to Les Jonquières. 'You said you wanted to have a look!'

'Of course,' Sylvia replies. 'Let's move on!' They ride to the far end of the beach, where Métèque is now rolling in the sand, and make a right to enter the woods from that side. Passing through the forest with its dappled sunshine, they race onward over a bridle path that is dangerously narrow at certain points. After a while, they reach the boundary of Les Jonquières, and before long the stone structure of the house shimmers through the trees. At a clearing, Sylvia stops and overlooks the area from the sloping hill. A severe storm downed a few trees on this spot some years ago, allowing them a good view of the solid stone house, the yard and the stables. They can see the *petite carrière*, the *grande carrière*, the horses in the pastures that are surrounded by the wooded area. 'Oh, that must be the new stable block,' Sylvia points in the direction of the property below. 'It's more obvious from here.'

'Yes,' Sébastien says. 'You know, I've never looked at Jonquières from this point. Good overall view.'

They make their way further down through the shady forest until the trees make way for the yard and they find themselves near the stables where they dismount. They leave their horses in the shade by the pasture and enter the house. Sylvia is delighted by the brightness of the kitchen. 'It looks just like when … when Natalie had it done.'

'That was my intention, Sylvia. Come, I'll show you the rest. It's been painted and cleaned, but all the rooms are still quite empty.'

They continue viewing the house that for Sylvia, too,

was her home after she married Pierre and her father almost disowned her for marrying him. Those were hard times, with Pierre's bankruptcy looming, but Monseigneur, the only remaining racehorse that Pierre owned, continued to win races and their troubles soon became a thing of the past. Sylvia's father, M. Lambert, grew milder towards his son-in-law and the 'bastard child' Sébastien, and he began visiting Les Jonquières regularly.

'The kitchen is the only liveable space at the moment,' Sébastien's voice interrupts Sylvia's reminiscing. 'Can I offer you something, coffee or wine?'

'Tea. Do you have tea?'

Sébastien sets about preparing the drink as Sylvia lets her eyes slide across the room. Apart from the new appliances, it looks almost exactly as it was in the days when Sébastien came to live here with his wife Natalie. Sylvia recognises the wooden table and chairs. The cushions are still in the shed at Fontenelle no doubt, and she understands that Sébastien needs to take his time moving back into the house where he once lived with Natalie. Sébastien puts the tea in front of his stepmother and places a few sweet rolls, which he found in a bag on the counter, beside it.

'*Merci*,' Sylvia says.

They hear footsteps approaching, and Sébastien turns to see Nicolas entering the kitchen. 'Morning, Nicolas. How's everything?'

'Good. Word must have spread as we had several people checking Les Jonquières out.'

'That's promising.'

'I left a list with a few phone numbers, of interested parties, on your desk.'

Sébastien gives him a surprised look. 'Desk? Since when do I have a desk?'

'Since we finished your office, patron.'

Sylvia has to smile at the last remark. 'Patron?' She remembers well that it had taken Sébastien some time before he called his own father 'papa'. He always referred to Pierre as 'patron' when he was a child, as he wasn't used to having someone he could refer to as his father.

Sébastien's curiosity is now aroused. 'Well, let's go and see.' Sylvia, too, is interested and follows the men outside. She has a hunch where this office might be situated, and her hunch is correct. It is located between the kitchen and the stables, where it has always been. Pierre used to use it as an office, even though it was a room where gear and saddles were stored as well. The freshly painted door opens into an office where the stone walls have remained the same for decades. It's the new desk with a chair that evokes the only contemporary feel in the room. The laptop computer and the telephone on the desk complete the result. Sébastien is satisfied. 'Perfect,' he says. 'Thank you, Nicolas.'

Sylvia strolls over to the stables and takes a look inside a few boxes. It is like old times to her, and she feels a sense of happiness and contentment, now that Sébastien is back on their familiar soil.

Stagnant streaky clouds hover in the skies above Nice, and the air is warm. The crowds around the racecourse are growing, and soon the area is teeming with people that have come to watch the horse races. Several are on their way to the ticket windows to place their bets as others are returning to their seats. While stable hands are tending to the horses in the enclosure, jockeys walk in and out of the weighing room, handing their saddles back to the stable lads and conversing with trainers and horse owners. Pierre is holding a horse by the lead and talks to one of the jockeys from La Fontenelle, giving him a few last-minute instructions. Sébastien is talking to Pierre's trainer, but then walks towards his father. He informs him that he will be joining Sylvia in the section of the stands reserved for horse owners. Some trucks are moving about slowly and are seeking a way to leave the area to park in the allocated spaces. Sébastien is absorbed by the hustle and bustle around the racecourse, something he was so familiar with in the past. He spots Sylvia and joins her and a few others of their acquaintance to wait for the race to begin. 'Have you been to the betting booths?' Sylvia asks him. Sébastien shakes his head. 'I've placed a bet on Flaming Star,' Sylvia says with a knowing look.

'He is a fantastic horse,' Sébastien acknowledges. One of the friends who is sitting in the row next to them stands up. 'I'll just be going down to get something to drink,' she says. 'Anyone else want something?'

'I wouldn't mind a cold orange juice. If it's no trouble,' Sylvia says.

'I'll fetch it,' Sébastien offers. 'What can I get you?' he asks the lady.

'Oh, that's kind of you. Could you get me a beer, please? A cold beer.' The rest of the small circle of friends declines, and Sébastien makes his way down from the seating area and through crowds of people. He's following the barrier along the race track and enters the outer area where the pavilion must be. He can't recall what would be the quickest way to get there. A bit further on, he sees his father and the trainer finding their way through the crowds and to the proprietors' tribune. Sébastien seeks to reach the pavilion. The people are dispersing, and many are on their way to the places from which they can watch the races. Sébastien walks hurriedly and sees the pavilion through the people who have not yet made their way to their vantage points. To save time and avoid the crowds, he walks between a couple of trucks that are parked here.

All at once, someone grabs him by the neck and pulls him out of public view. Before he knows what is happening, he feels a gush of pain across his face, and he's on the ground. Sébastien tries to ward off the unknown force, but his face is pressed into the dirt, cutting off his breath. His arms grab behind him, and he feels some fabric between his fingers, but another blow from the attacker causes him to lose his grasp.

'Morgan!' The voice cuts through the noises around him and the unknown force releases the grip on him slightly. 'Morgan! Don't even think it! Let go of him!' Sébastien feels the man relax the hold he has on him and move away. He tries to turn onto his back and sees someone's feet approach from where he lies. When he glances up, he perceives Jules Garnier. His hands are holding a gun tightly, and it is aimed straight at the criminal's face.

'Back away from him,' Jules demands. 'Sébastien, on your feet.'

With an aching head and spitting dirt, Sébastien manages to roll on all fours while he tries to stand up.

'Turn around, Morgan. And don't let me tell you twice,' Jules hisses through his teeth while indicating with his gun to move it. Morgan turns and holds both his hands up against one of the trucks. Jules kicks him in the insides of his knees, and the criminal stumbles and falls to the ground. Morgan's furious face looks up at him. 'You bloody bastard.'

Sébastien shakes his dizzy head, still not quite sure what has just happened. He sits down on the ground, leaning his back against a large tyre of one of the trucks.

'I've been following that annoying bastard,' Jules

tells him. 'I was surprised he went to the races today, but then I saw you here as well.' Jules notices a few security guards and calls out to them. When the men are near, Jules takes out his licence and shows it to them. 'He's a criminal,' pointing to Morgan who is still on the ground, 'and he was in the process of beating up this man.'

The security guards grab Morgan by his shoulder and pull him on his feet. '*Bien*. You'd better come with us.' They tie Morgan's hands together. 'You two need to come as well.'

One of Sébastien's eyes starts to swell, and he feels his face hurting.

'We will. But first, I've to take him to First Aid,' Jules tells the security guards.' He holds out his hand to help Sébastien to his feet.

'Over there,' one of the guards indicates. 'Near the entrance. And afterwards, you come straight to the *poste de police*.' They each grab Morgan by an arm and lead him away.

'How are you?' Jules asks Sébastien who is still sitting on the ground. Sébastien grabs his hand and pulls himself up. Blood has started dripping from a graze on his cheek.

'Let's have that fixed,' Jules says. 'I'm sorry, *copain*. I'd no idea he was out to be violent.'

Sébastien is pleased Jules showed up at all. 'Thanks, Jules. It could've been much worse. Let's go.'

They walk across the terrain until they see the *premiers secours* unit. They enter, and wait for a child with a scraped knee who is being rewarded with a sweet but apart from that, Sébastien is the only casualty and he is helped instantly. His wound is cleaned and cared for, and he is given a cream to help bring the swelling around his eye down. 'Right, monsieur Maréchal, you'll be as good as new in a few days,' the male nurse tells him and offers him the customary painkillers.

'*Merci*,' Sébastien says. '*Bien*. Jules, let's go to the police post, get that over and done with.'

The police unit is not far, and they enter the small office, which nonetheless carries all the equipment needed for emergencies. There's no sign of Morgan. Jules elaborates on the incident that took place a little over thirty minutes ago. A policewoman takes all the details down, and when both men have signed their statement, they make their way outside. Sébastien is disappointed that he has now missed the race in which one of his father's best horses showed his abilities. He suggests they should join the family.

'I noticed Pierre,' Jules says. 'But I was after Morgan.'

Outside, the crowd leaves their seats, and before long the terrain is swarming with people again. The race Sébastien came to see is now over.

Sylvia is the first to spot Sébastien while Pierre is walking down to the track to join his horse and jockey.

'Sébastien!' Sylvia is horrified. 'What happened? Have you had a fall?' She holds his arm and has a look at his face. 'We were wondering why you didn't come back.'

Jules glances at Sébastien but refrains from revealing the true cause of Sébastien's injury.

'Sylvia, have you ever met Jules?' Sébastien asks her. 'He's an old friend of Papa's.'

'Yes, but it's been a long while,' Sylvia replies. 'Bonjour. Pierre is down there, by his horse,' before turning her attention to Sebastien again. 'How did it happen? Did you stumble?'

'Uh, yes, you could say that. Sylvia, how did Papa's horse do?'

'He came in second, but Pierre is pleased,' Sylvia replies. 'The horse is young still.'

Jules follows Pierre's movements down by the tracks. 'Let's meet him,' Sébastien suggests. Sylvia casts a worried glance as she watches the two men walking down.

On this sultry evening, the family have made themselves comfortable in the yard at Les Jonquières. Jules, who came back with them after the races had finished, is sitting between them. Nicolas and a few men in Pierre's employ have moved some of Sébastien's furniture back to the property, and garden chairs and benches are a convenient addition on this warm summer's evening.

It has come to their knowledge that Gilbert Morgan is now being held in custody, but Jules has his doubts. 'For him that's routine by now. I don't know how he does it, but he always manages to talk his way out of situations like these.'

'Not any more,' Pierre says. 'I'll put my lawyers on this. I've had it with that man.'

Sylvia exits the house holding a tray with snacks and places it on the garden table. Quietly, she sits down next to Pierre. She was shocked to learn that is was Morgan who had caused her son's battered face.

'It still puzzles me, what his dealings are with certain men within the police force,' Jules says. 'That's why I've been following Morgan. Day and night I was on his tail these past few days … a hard time. I'm getting too old for this.'

'I'm sorry, Jules,' Pierre apologises, 'but at least it is starting to pay off now.'

'You said that your informant was undercover,' Sébastien now joins in the conversation. 'Dealing with this Morgan.'

'That is what he told me. But when I was tailing Morgan, he met with the man twice, and to me it looked like they were partners in crime more than anything else. As if … as if Morgan had *bought* this man. And I have a photo to prove it.'

'A photo?' Pierre is curious.

'Where Morgan hands my informer money.'

'Then we have a case,' Sébastien says. 'That's bribery.'

Sylvia sips her wine while all the time listening to the men discussing the situation. 'He might have handed that money to his superiors,' she now says. 'He might truly be undercover.'

Jules nods. 'That may be the case.' He takes a sip from his coffee. 'But I find that hard to believe.'

Sébastien finishes his glass of wine and pours another. 'And the man who met Morgan in Marseille, that day when I took François back. Have you found anything on him?'

Jules shakes his head. 'Nothing. And I haven't seen him with Morgan at all.' He takes an olive from the plate and pops it in his mouth. 'To be honest, I don't know who I can trust any more in the police force.'

Pierre knows Jules to be a trustworthy and reliable man. It must be a disappointment to him to have to deal with people who don't turn out to be on the straight and narrow. 'First thing tomorrow morning I'll get in touch with my lawyer,' he says. 'I don't care what else that Morgan has done, but I won't let him beat up a son of mine.' He nods in Sébastien's direction. 'He will pay for this.'

'And the arson attacks. He must be behind those, too,' Jules concludes. 'I hope evidence of that will be found soon.'

'Someone might come forward who knows something about it,' Sébastien says, but Jules remains sceptical. 'That car thief must have done it. I'm sure of it,' Jules replies. 'Highly unlikely he will come forward though. Likely he already has a criminal record and is not keen to have another offence added to that.'

The warm evening breeze wafts the scent of lavender and dried grass their way, while somewhere frogs croak in a brook. The horses that have found a new life at Les Jonquières are heard shuffling their hooves in the pasture. During their conversation, the stars above have become more intense in the now deep, dark sky where a crescent moon shines brightly. Jules checks his watch. 'I must be off, he says. 'I aimed to go back to Marseille today if I hadn't spotted Morgan in Nice … ' he gets up from the table, 'and my curiosity got the better of me.'

'Stay,' Pierre says. 'You can stay at Fontenelle, with us. Drive back tomorrow, during the day.'

Jules is hesitant. 'Please,' Sylvia says. 'You must be tired. You can have a good night's rest before you drive back.'

Even though Jules doesn't like to be a burden to people, his fatigue overcomes his reluctance and he gives in. They will all return to La Fontenelle, and Sylvia begins to clear the table with Sébastien lending her a hand.

In the morning, Sébastien is the last one to rise. When he rolls out of his bed and has a look in the mirror, he must acknowledge that his face has seen better days, but at least the pain has diminished. He freshens up under the powerful stream of the shower and gets dressed in jeans and a thin T-shirt. Downstairs, the kitchen is empty, and he tries the study, but there is no sign of his father. When he leaves the house, the summer sun is already high in the sky, and he squints because of its brightness. An action that doesn't exactly agree with his black eye. Sébastien walks towards the training track when he finds no one at the stables. In front of him, he sees the *parcour* through the trees, shimmering in the sun. The horses' hooves hit the ground with dull thuds and jockeys, bent forward in their saddles, spur them on. While the heat beats down on the track, the horses seem to have trouble keeping their pace. Sébastien notices his father with the trainer in the middle of the track keeping a watchful eye on the horses' progress. He ducks underneath the fencing to join them. His father waves at him. 'Bonjour. How are you?' When Sébastien is near, Pierre looks at his face. 'Feeling better?'

'Yeah, fine. Jules gone home?'

'He left early. I think he is eager to get to the bottom of this Morgan business.' Pierre follows the horses' running their circles, and he shakes his head. 'The heat is bothering them. We'll cut it short for today.'

'Have you been in touch with your lawyer?' Sébastien wonders.

'If you have time, we can go there this afternoon. We have to bring this case before a judge.'

That sounds somewhat drastic to Sébastien.

'It's not just the violence, Sébastien. His actions could have caused major fires in this area,' Pierre says. 'There's enough to have him convicted.'

'But there is no proof that he was connected to these fires at all.'

Pierre draws his eyes away from his horses and looks at his son. 'Well, that's for the police to find out,' he says, to then address the trainer again. 'Shall we call it a day? It's unusually hot, and not even noon yet.'

His trainer agrees. 'You're right. They can't seem to

move their legs.' He calls out to the jockeys to stop, and one by one the horses come to a halt. 'Take them back, men. It's been enough for today.'

With their nostrils flared the horses slow down to a walking pace. In motion with the movement of their gait, their heads move back and forth. The poor animals are glistening with sweat. Most of the jockeys dismount and walk beside their horse. Sébastien follows his father and the trainer back to the yard, and as stable hands start tending to the horses, Pierre and Sébastien walk over to the house. In the kitchen, Sébastien starts preparing something to eat as he has missed *le petit-déjeuner*. Pierre disappears into his study. A while later he returns to the kitchen, where Sébastien is just finishing his meal. He places a folder on the table. 'This is all the proof Jules left. We can hand it to the lawyer,' he says.

On the way to the lawyers' offices, it has become clear that Pierre has no intention of letting the case rest until justice has been done. Sébastien is currently standing by the window in M. Auberge's office, looking down onto the street where people are going about their daily routines, while his father is discussing the occurrences that happened at Les Jonquières. And he doesn't mince his words about yesterday's incident. Sébastien turns away from the window and goes to his seat to join them. He has refrained from taking off his sunglasses because the looks that people give him are starting to annoy him.

'OK, Pierre. So, you've brought charges against him,' his lawyer says. 'Is this Morgan now in police custody?'

'As far as we know,' Sébastien replies.

'What is the likelihood they let him out on bail?' Pierre wants to know.

'I think that's unlikely, not with his track record,' M.

Auberge says.

'Fine, but it looks like he has friends *within* the police force,' Pierre objects. 'What if they let him slip through the net again?'

'That's not certain, Papa. Jules is still working on that,' Sébastien says.

Pierre looks at him. 'He's a criminal, Sébastien. He knows how the system works.' Pierre's face turns dark, and he sounds annoyed. 'He's been trying to destroy Sébastien's property and now he just comes out of nowhere and beats him up!'

'Pierre, leave it to me,' monsieur Auberge says. 'I'll work on it and we'll make sure he stays behind bars.' He stands up. 'Now, I still have a lot to do. If you don't mind,' and he walks to the door to see the two men out.

'Thank you, monsieur Auberge.' Sébastien shakes his hand as they leave, and he follows his father outside. 'That was a short visit,' Pierre says. 'It was as if he didn't want to listen to everything we had to say.'

'Papa, he has all the information he needs, don't worry about it. And I'm sure he is a busy man.'

Pierre agrees. 'He's busy because he's a good lawyer.'

Since his stay in the hospital, Pierre has regarded riding less important, but now he has decided to saddle one of his horses and ride with his son to Les Jonquières. He follows Sébastien on Jeune Homme along the bridle path. They take the route they so often took when they rode together in the days when Sébastien and his small family lived at Jonquières. They find their way through the forest, pass the Fairy Tree on the green divide and move onward to Les Jonquières. Upon arriving, they notice that the usually tranquil and hushed area surrounding the house and stables, is now unusually crowded. A group of schoolchildren with a teacher crowd the yard, and by one of the stable blocks a truck and horse trailer are parked. Nicolas is near the office, talking to an unfamiliar person. As Pierre and Sébastien dismount, the children rush towards them, and in no time they are surrounded. Sébastien is surprised while Pierre is somewhat apprehensive. 'Why are these children here? Shouldn't they be in school?'

'School assignment,' the teacher says, and he points in the direction of Nicolas. 'Your man said it was alright if we had a look around.'

Sébastien assents. 'That's fine,' and he and Pierre walk over to Nicolas.

'Hello, patron. New customer,' he introduces the man standing beside him. 'Monsieur Lemoine.'

Pierre instantly recognises the immaculately dressed man with the tanned face and his grey hair in perfect trim. 'Paul-Jean! It has been a long time. How are you?'

'Pierre, good to see you,' the man replies.

'Are you dropping off one of your horses?' Pierre wonders. He motions towards the truck.

'Yes, my champion First in Line.'

'Is that so. Has he stopped racing? I remember seeing him on the course a few years ago.'

'He had a fall,' Paul-Jean says. 'He hasn't been the same so now we're retiring him.'

Sébastien interrupts the amicable conversation. 'When did they show up?' he asks Nicolas, referring to the schoolchildren.

'They're from the village school,' Nicolas replies. 'The teacher called, wanted to show them the retirement home for horses. Some have signed up for your riding classes, too.'

'Have they?' Sébastien says before he turns his attention to his new customer. 'Have you seen the facilities?'

'Yes, Nicolas showed me. It looks good what you have here. Pierre, at first I thought it was you starting this business. Maréchal, a familiar name in the world of horse racing.'

'No,' Pierre replies. 'It's my son here, taking on that challenge. I still train horses.'

'No retirement for you then,' Paul-Jean concludes.

Pierre shakes his head. 'But I am slowing down.' Sébastien glances at his father with a reserved look in his eyes. 'Would you mind stepping into my office?' he then says. Sébastien lets the man proceed as they enter his office. Paul-Jean is intrigued by Sébastien's black eye. 'What happened to you? Did you fall off a horse?'

'It was a fall,' Sébastien replies, 'but not off a horse.' He takes out the necessary papers and hands them to the man. 'When you've finished reading, you can sign it. On the dotted line,' he can't resist adding. He wishes the swelling and his black eye would fade, back to normal. Paul-Jean Lemoine looks at him as if desiring an explanation for the somewhat misplaced remark, before drawing his eyes towards the forms in front of him. He quickly and efficiently comes to the conclusion that all is in perfect order and he signs. 'I'm sure First in Line will be well looked after here, in a Maréchal stable.' Sébastien shakes Paul-Jean Lemoine's hand. 'That's one thing I can promise you.' The men walk outside where they join Nicolas. Pierre is strolling around by the stables to have another look at the property that his son has restored. He does not elaborate on what he sees, but his demeanour shows he is extremely pleased that Les Jonquières has become a property to be proud of again.

Marseille comes in his view, and the city appears moody and miserable with dark clouds threatening overhead. When Sébastien crosses its city limits, the surroundings have turned as dark as night. Without notice, the heavens open and the downpour slashes through the streets. Sébastien closes the windows of his car, and the windscreen-wipers sweep ferociously back and forth. They can hardly keep the rainwater from his car windows. Before long, the roads resemble streams, flowing with water. He tries to distinguish the streets and more by instinct than logic, he makes his way to the area he is looking for. He searches for a place to park closer to the building but has to resort to a spot across the street where he had parked on an earlier occasion. He grabs his fitness bag from the backseat and sweeps his jacket over his head when he gets out of the car. He locks the doors as he runs across to the fitness centre, his feet splashing through rainwater. He quickly dodges out of the rain and into the building. Inside, he shakes the wetness from his attire and goes over to the reception desk that is now occupied by a different young woman. 'Bonjour,' he is welcomed.

'Bonjour,' Sébastien says. 'I understand it's possible to get a day-pass? I'd like one, for today.'

'*Mais oui*, monsieur.' The young lady reaches in a drawer and takes out a small card.

'I was a member of this club once, in Paris,' he informs the girl. 'I thought I might try this one.'

The young woman looks at him. 'In that case, what is your name, Sir? I could check in the computer.'

'Maréchal. Sébastien Maréchal.' Sébastien looks around the hall while the receptionist checks the information relating to his past membership. He notices more members have found their way to the confinement of the space behind the glass wall.

'Oh yes,' the young woman says. 'You cancelled your subscription about four years ago.'

'That's right.'

'Have you thought about rejoining?'

'No. I just want to try a few of your classes.'

The woman looks at him with anticipation. 'We have a special offer at the moment.'

'No, thank you. In any case, I don't live in Marseille.'

'I can give you a discount just the same, since you were a member. That'll be fifteen Euros.'

Sébastien takes out his bank card and puts it in the device. When he has paid, he removes the program, which he has taken a few weeks ago, from his pocket. 'Where is this class taking place?' he asks.

'Oh, that one is in studio two. That's up the stairs, to your left,' the young woman informs him. 'Male changing rooms are down there through that door and into the corridor.'

'Thank you.' Sébastien takes his fitness bag and, following the directions, walks over to the corridor. In no time at all, he has changed into gear that, for a while, he was accustomed to wearing when training. It was mainly Angéline who was the regular fitness goer. He merely went along to please her.

He is not the only early arrival in the studio where the class will take place, a few women are setting up their gear as well. In an effort to be inconspicuous, he finds a spot in the back of the room and begins taking out the equipment he was familiar with four years ago. Slowly but surely, more members are arriving, and they too are taking steps, weights and bars for the afternoon class. It dawns on him that he is the only male there.

With quick steps, the instructor enters the room and

begins to prepare for the lesson she is about to teach. As he takes a few sips of water from his bottle, Sébastien wonders if he should make himself known to Cécile, but decides she will notice soon enough.

Cécile begins to explain the exercise when the music for the first track sounds. She looks around the room when suddenly her eyes are locked onto his face and for a moment she forgets her task. Sébastien gives her a subtle smile as he follows her instructions.

'Sorry, I forgot to ask,' Cécile then addresses the class, 'is there anyone new here today?' and, looking towards her father at the back: 'You are familiar with this training?'

Sébastien nods, '*oui*,' at the same time he finds it odd that his daughter treats him as if he is a stranger to her. The lesson continues, and Sébastien pays close attention to his daughter's instructions as she also participates, to illustrate the way the exercises should be done. He feels admiration for his daughter's teaching abilities and he must admit she is a fine instructor. Now and then she walks through the class to explain to women here and there the best technique for the different exercises. When she's near him, she merely watches, but she remains professional. Sébastien begins to feel awkward, and thinks he might have made a mistake coming here, invading her life in this way. He is careful not to blunder his way through the training exercises.

Cooldown is imminent, and Sébastien realises that his physical strength is not what it once was. When the abdominal exercises are finished and the cooldown is complete, he follows the others and clears away his gear, as is the custom. Most of the women have left the studio when Sébastien walks over to Cécile. She is briefly in conversation with someone else but then turns to him.

'You teach a great class, Cécile. Thank you.'

Sébastien finds the look she gives him somewhat condescending. 'Is that what you came here for? To see me teach?' his daughter asks.

'I was curious,' Sébastien says. 'And now, I'm also impressed.' He looks at her. 'Cécile, I came because I wanted to show interest in what you do. Is that so strange?'

'Grab your bag,' she demands. 'We can talk downstairs.'

Sébastien follows in his daughter's energetic stride as they walk down the stairs and into the small eatery where Cécile takes out a few cold drinks, and they sit down.

'I hope you don't mind me showing up here,' Sébastien says, sounding apologetic.

Cécile looks at him. 'I was a bit surprised, to say the least. You, in a fitness studio?' She can't suppress a smile.

'Didn't you know that Angéline and I were members in Paris?'

'Yes, but I also know that for you it didn't last long. You didn't like it.'

Sébastien sips his cold drink. 'I prefer training outside, in the fresh air. On horseback.'

'Yes, Papa, that is where our differences lie,' Cécile informs him.

'We can't all have the same interests,' Sébastien admits. 'But.' He stops for a moment. 'I would like it if you'd come home more often.'

'I live here, Papa. Our home is here.' Her glance has fallen on the yellowing skin around her father's eye. 'What's that yellow around your eye?'

'Oh, that.' Subconsciously he touches his face. 'I had a black eye. It's better now.'

Cécile becomes more serious. 'Papa, what is it you

want me to do? I can't just give up everything I've worked for here.'

'I understand that. And that's not what I'm asking of you, but ... we haven't been on the best footing. I blame myself for that, for the neglect and ... and not being there for you.'

Cécile places her hand on his arm. 'There was no neglect, Papa. Mamie and Grand-père were always there for me. I appreciate better now, the reason why you stayed away. Why you had a hard time living in the house ... after Maman passed away.'

Sébastien turns his head away from her. He has a sudden insight into the issues that have bothered him through the years. A feeling comes over him. A feeling that there never was a wedge between him and his daughter. The way they are sitting here, talking, being friendly and familiar with each other. Only now does it become clear to him that his daughter has possibly always sought to connect with him, but it must have been the distance that he created himself that had made her insecure and distant towards him.

'Papa?'

'Yes. I think you're right,' he quickly replies. 'I mean, I'm glad you understand.' He looks at her. 'You know the door at Les Jonquières is always open. You can always come home.'

Cécile nods. 'I know that, Papa.'

'So, how's Thomas? Is he in school when you're working?'

'He's in preschool,' Cécile says. 'Which reminds me, I've to go and pick him up!' She quickly grabs her bag and shoots up from her chair. 'Oh God. Now I'm late.'

Sébastien stands up also and catches her arm, 'Cécile,' before he kisses her on the cheek. For a moment, the young woman seems embarrassed, but then places a kiss on her father's cheek. 'You can come and visit us too, you know,' she says and is out the door.

Sébastien is slow to follow. He refrains from going to the changing rooms to change back into his usual clothes and leaves the building still wearing his fitness attire. By this time, there is no sign of his daughter. He glances up at the dark sky where now streaks of blue appear. The surfaces are still wet, and some raindrops are spitting in his face when he walks across the street to his car. He gets in, and as he puts the key in the ignition, a contented feeling creeps up on him.

At Les Jonquières the men are busy unloading the last pieces of furniture that came from the shed at La Fontenelle. Sébastien is walking through the rooms upstairs to convince himself how well it all looks, newly decorated and now furnished. He goes down the stairs to the hall where, in the living-room, a few women are cleaning familiar pieces of furniture. Sylvia wasn't having it when he suggested throwing them away. He agrees, the furniture does give the room a sense of benign familiarity.

When the truck has been emptied of its content and everything is in its place inside the house, the women start engaging themselves in the kitchen to come out with salads, cheese, bread and the 'devastatingly delicious' wine that Michèl Beauchamp has brought with him. It doesn't take long for everyone to find a seat around the table in the yard and enjoy the tasty lunch. Sébastien turns his head when he hears a car approach on the dirt road.

'More help at hand, patron,' Julien informs him as he cuts a piece off the cheese.

'There's enough food for everybody,' Nicolas's wife says.

'You always get those who show up when the work's done,' Raymond offers.

The car speeds into the yard and stops somewhere opposite the stables. Sébastien is surprised to see that it is his brother getting out of the car. He stands up and walks over to meet him. 'François!' Sébastien greets his brother. 'A surprise arrival!' The men embrace each other as the door on the passenger side opens as well, and Madeleine gets out. 'You're just in time for lunch,' Sébastien says. 'Have you been to see Papa and Maman?'

'We were on our way there, but I was curious about Les Jonquières. So, thought we'd stop off here first.'

Few introductions are needed when Sébastien's brother and niece join the others. More chairs are placed around the table, and they continue their meal.

'How long are you staying?' Sébastien asks his brother.

'Summer break at uni has started, and I've postponed my next research trip.' François takes a gulp from his glass. 'Sébastien, the house is sold. I'm still looking for something else.'

'I'm sure Papa and Sylvia won't mind having you around for the summer,' Sébastien says.

'That's what I thought. So, summer holidays at La Fontenelle. That'll be a change.'

François always has a knack of being ironic when in adversity. Sébastien nods towards Madeleine, who has started a conversation with Nicolas's wife. 'Will she live with you, or Louise?'

'She stays with me. No matter how much pressure Louise puts on her, she refuses to live with her mother.' He dips a chunk of bread in the potato salad on his plate. 'Louise wasn't home a lot these past few years. Madeleine has become used to having me around,' he justifies his daughter's reasoning, but Sébastien has a hunch it is Louise's attitude that drove her children away from her.

'More wine anyone?' Michèl offers. Glasses are lifted and filled while Madeleine helps herself to the mineral water on the table.

'It will be nice to have a summer that doesn't overflow with stressful situations,' François says. 'I'm sick of that.' He slings an arm around his brother's shoulders. 'We can go riding together again. Like we used to.' Sébastien feels the same, but his thoughts drift to his daughter and grandson, who are not part of the scene he currently sees around him.

The soft summer drizzle that descends on Les Jonquières brings a welcome coolness from the heat of the past week. The fine rain brings the flowers and trees back from their slumber. The horses in their boxes are showing their heads through the doors and sniff the fresh air while Sébastien is scraping dirty straw out of their shelter and replacing it with a fresh, clean layer. The smell of a horse's stable beats the smell of city fumes a hundred times over, he finds. When he has finished his daily tasks, he places the broom, shovel and pitchfork back in the tool storage. He grabs the wheelbarrow with the last bit of dirty straw and takes it to the disposal heap at the back of the stable blocks. He returns to the yard and walks into his office where he has coffee percolating. He lifts his head when he hears a car approach and stop outside, near the house. Through the open door, he sees his father and Jules Garnier leave the car behind them and walk towards the kitchen door. 'Over here!' Sebastien says in a loud voice. Jules and Pierre change direction and enter the office. 'Bonjour, Sébastien,' Jules says.

'Morning. Are there any new developments?'

Sebastien is curious to know.

'Sébastien,' Pierre greets his son. 'Ah, I see you have the coffee ready.' He instantly goes about pouring a few cups and places them on the desk.

Jules hands Sebastien a folder with his findings. 'Here's some more proof for the lawyer,' he says. 'Now, here's what's going on. Morgan was released on bail – '

'What!' Sébastien is appalled and looks in his father's direction.

'That was news to me, too, son.'

' … but he has been arrested, again. The man you saw him with in Marseille, is now an undercover policeman. I didn't know that,' Jules says, 'and once he had gathered enough proof to nail that … Morgan, the police moved in and arrested him. The only reason why he had Jonquières in mind to use as a development was to launder money he had accumulated from drug trafficking.'

'Papa, didn't you say he had a deal with a bank?'

'Lies!' Jules calls out. 'All lies. And Pierre here, almost fell for his scheme. Like others have done.'

Sébastien lowers himself onto the desk chair. 'And what about your informer?'

'Well, that's a bit of a sensitive situation,' Jules goes on. 'I've learned that he was undercover but, I now have a problem trusting him. I believe he was Morgan's informer as well, and it's never a good thing when the enemy knows about your plans.'

'Morgan's in custody now,' Pierre says. 'He can't cause any more trouble.'

Jules shakes his head. 'You're old school, Pierre. That's not how things work these days.'

'What do you mean?' Sébastien says sharply. 'Don't say they'll let him go again.'

'I hope not,' Jules continues, 'but I believe he might

have gathered information he could use against us. Morgan was on good terms with my informer. He might've let the odd bit of information slip.'

Pierre paces up and down the office and now stands still in front of Jules. 'And what if there is evidence that can be used against *him*?'

'That has crossed my mind. And I hope, I truly hope, that the police are smart enough to search my informer's house,' Jules adds with a significant look, 'and hope they will find evidence. Otherwise ... ' Jules shrugs his shoulders.

'And what does all this mean for us?' Sébastien asks. 'We have filed complaints. We're suing him for assault and damages and – '

'Morgan will have to appear in court, there's no doubt,' Jules interrupts. 'Question is, to what extent will he be associated with the arson attacks. What sentence will he get?'

Pierre starts his restless pacing again. 'What is wrong with this world? Are we ruled by criminals?'

Sébastien rises from his chair and walks over to the open door. 'We will demand that the police search that man's house. We'll demand that the car that was stolen is forensically examined.'

Jules agrees. 'That is your right.'

'I found it strange that the car was returned to its rightful owner so quickly,' Sébastien says. 'God knows what the police have overlooked.'

Jules walks over to him. 'I know they've had forensics check it.'

'And?'

'They found some items that could lead to the person who stole the car, but that's all,' Jules says. He shrugs his shoulders. 'There is a chance that this car thief will be caught and who knows? Maybe he will talk, to save his own skin.'

'Let's hope he does, if he is found,' Pierre says. 'The more evidence against Morgan, the better.'

'I couldn't agree more,' Jules says. 'Well, Pierre, Sébastien. I must be off.' He walks out the door towards his car, leaving Sébastien and his father behind.

'Point is, we're not much wiser,' Pierre says as he stands next to Sébastien.

'He's tried his best, Papa. I'm sure he is limited in how much he is allowed to do.' They watch the car disappear from their view. Only the settling dust remains.

At La Fontenelle's beach, the waves roll upon its shore as horses' hooves hit the water's edge. François and Sébastien have given their mother a head start, and now race to catch up with her, but they haven't taken Sylvia's riding skills into account. Instead of gaining ground, the distance between her and her sons becomes wider, and she reaches the forest at Les Jonquières by half a lap. When she turns her horse around, she laughs when she sees her sons have failed to show off their ability to win.

'OK, Maman. You win,' François pants when they reach her.

'I told you, François,' his brother says. 'You have to train harder if you want to beat Maman!'

François's panting prevents him from commenting on Sébastien's remark.

'Have you been breathing properly, François?' his older brother asks him. 'It's not normal to be out of breath like this. Even your horse has caught his breath already!'

Sylvia jumps down from her saddle to sit down on a rock by the shrubs. 'We'd better wait awhile, for François to recover.' She hugs his shoulder when her son sits down next to her.

Sébastien allows his horse a breather as well and lowers himself onto the sand.

'I'm so glad you both have come home,' Sylvia expresses, and her glance wanders to the rolling waves of the Mediterranean. 'Just like old times.'

Sébastien concurs. 'There's something comforting about returning to home soil.'

François agrees. 'But I love my work. For us it'll only be for the summer holidays.'

'What if your father wants to stop working and enjoy his retirement?' Sylvia says. 'Would you then come home for good, François?'

'Maman, the horses *are* his retirement. Papa will never stop doing what he loves most.'

Sébastien agrees. 'Papa likes to believe he is slowing down, but he hasn't slowed down one bit.'

A soft rustling in the shrubs behind them manifests the large white dog, and he walks their way. Sébastien calls him over and pets him on the side. 'It's incredible how independent Métèque is. He just wanders around the whole area as if he's king of the jungle.'

Sylvia strokes the dog as well. 'He is a king,' she says. 'A very clever king, aren't you, Métèque.' The dog takes it in his stride and lies down between them. 'Everyone's friend,' Sébastien says and gives him a good rub. François looks at the scene, and a subtle smile plays around his lips. He then gets up and grabs his horse's rein. 'Shall we go?'

'I thought you were on holiday, François. Why the rush?' his mother wonders.

'Sorry, force of habit.'

Sylvia rises from the rock as well. 'Slow down, darling. You're home now, in the countryside. Forget your busy life for a while.'

Holding their horses by the lead allows for a slower pace as they stroll back to La Fontenelle. Métèque follows them behind and walks with them until he decides on a shorter way back to the village.

After a pleasant morning at La Fontenelle, Sébastien's work at his 'retirement home' draws him back to Les Jonquières. Twelve horses are now stabled here, and he expects two more arrivals in the coming week.

He only finds Nicolas there, busy mucking out the stables. Sébastien takes a wheelbarrow and helps him clear away the dirty straw. 'That was the last one,' Nicolas says. Sébastien disposes of the manure, and walks back to the yard where Nicolas has found a seat on the bench to rest. Sébastien joins him there. Nicolas hands him a cold drink, and together they enjoy the sounds of nature around them. A breeze gently moves the canopies of the trees around the house, while some birds have braved the warmth and sing the odd song in the branches. Sébastien watches the horses in the distance, relaxing and grazing in the shade of a few trees. Thomas's pony is among them, a bit shorter on his feet than the racehorses who stand higher on their legs.

'Well, I'd better be off,' Nicolas says when he has finished his drink. 'I can come again on Thursday, if you need me.'

'That's fine.' Sébastien follows him towards the house, and while he is about to go in, Nicolas walks over to his car and drives off. Sébastien waves at him as the car disappears behind a few bushes. Inside the house, he checks his fridge for something edible, but he now discerns that because of his many visits to La Fontenelle, he has neglected purchasing provisions for his own household. That was something he was hardly used to when he lived in Paris. They ate out a lot, and it was mainly Angéline who made sure the fridge was always full.

The sound of a car outside has him wondering if Nicolas has forgotten something, but when he looks out the window, he sees it is a small yellow car that has driven up. He remembers the unpleasant incident the last time he saw that car in his yard. Slowly, he makes his way towards the door and takes his time to open it.

The car door on the passenger side flies open, and Thomas comes running towards the house. 'Grandpapa!' Sébastien opens the door wider and steps outside. 'Thomas?' The boy stops in front of him, a smile from ear to ear on his face. 'Grandpapa.'

'Hello, Thomas,' are the only words Sébastien can find to say. Thomas holds out his arms for his grandfather to pick him up. He lifts the boy into his arms, and Thomas's small hands clutch around his neck. Cécile is standing by the car and waves at him. 'Hello, Papa!'

Only now does Sébastien see the suitcases that she is lifting from the back of her small car. 'Cécile,' he manages to say in his astonishment. Holding his grandson, he walks over to her.

'Hello, Papa,' Cécile reiterates and kisses her father on his cheek. 'I hope you won't mind having us around for a while.'

'No, of course not.'

Cécile notices his bewilderment. 'I've been thinking about what you said, and when there was an opening at the branch in Nice, I asked for a transfer.'

'What do you mean?'

'I'll start my job in Nice, next week, is what I mean, Papa. But, I'm still looking for a place to live. So, then I thought of you, wanting us to come home more often ... So, here we are.'

Sébastien's facial expression changes from astonishment to gladness. 'And Maman will let me ride my pony,' Thomas adds to his mother's account.

'Really?' Sébastien looks at his daughter.

'Yes. Well, we don't all have the same interests, Papa.' She picks up the two suitcases and starts to walk to the house.

'Here, let me help you.' He puts Thomas on the ground in order to take the luggage from her. Thomas has spotted his pony in the paddock, but his mother stops him when he wants to run towards the animal. 'Let's settle in first, Thomas. You'll have plenty of time for your pony while we're here.'

They enter the house and Sébastien puts the suitcases on the floor. 'I'm sorry, but I just noticed I don't have much food in the house. I'll have to get some things.'

'Don't worry about that. Now, where do you want us?' Cécile asks.

'Uhm ... Well, I suppose Thomas can have your old room, and you. Just take your pick, most rooms upstairs are unoccupied.' He takes the suitcases and proceeds to the hall. 'You're lucky, I only had all the furniture moved here last week,' Sébastien informs her as they follow Thomas who is flying up the stairs ahead of them.

Cécile is surprised. 'Is that so? I thought you'd settled back in ages ago ... The one on the end, Thomas.'

Thomas opens the door to the room where his mother slept as a small child. It is now freshly decorated, but for the bed, desk and chair that were in storage in the shed for over twenty years.

'Gosh,' Cécile utters. 'Have you kept all that?' She walks over to the bed she slept in as a child and sits down.

'It does have a new mattress,' Sébastien says. Thomas jumps on the bed as well. 'Oh!' he then remembers. 'Maman, I have to show Grandpapa!' and he starts pulling at one of the suitcases.

'What do you mean?' Cécile wants to know.

'My riding cap!' Thomas excitedly pulls at the lock on the suitcase. His mother lends a hand, and soon a sturdy children's riding helmet appears from under children's shirts and pants. Thomas grabs it from his mother's hand and holds it up for his grandfather to see. 'Look Grandpapa! When I wear this, I can always ride my pony!'

'Then we have to make sure you wear it.' Sébastien takes the helmet from him for a closer inspection.

'These are specially approved for children,' Cécile says. 'I don't want him on any horse, unless he wears it.'

Sébastien looks at her. 'You can count on it. Thank you, Cécile.'

His daughter stands up from the bed. 'Right. Thomas, let's find Mummy's room.'

One look in her father's fridge had been enough for Cécile to jump in her car and return only when she had purchased enough groceries to fill it. Currently, she is laying the table in the yard and placing the dishes for their evening meal on it. A soft breeze wafts cooling air on this warm evening, and it carries the spicy scents of honeysuckle and lavender that grow near the house. Her son has spent the time with his grandfather and his pony almost from the moment they arrived, but now it is time for them to sit down for dinner, and she calls the two over.

Sébastien sits down next to Thomas while Cécile puts the food on their plate. 'Thank you, Cécile.' He looks her way. 'I really appreciate your care, but I do want you to know, you don't have to do this every day.'

'It's fine, Papa. I'm glad to do it.'

Thomas does not loiter and starts eating so fast that it surprises his mother. 'Thomas, don't gobble your food down.'

'He must be hungry,' her father says.

'That'll be a first,' but she can't ignore the fact that Thomas stopped eating well since the last time he stayed with his great-grandparents at La Fontenelle. The silence that follows is not for the lack of conversation, but for the tasty food Cécile has prepared. Thomas scraping his plate and finishing his drink is an indication to Cécile that she made the right decision by coming back to stay with her father.

'Papa, there's something I wanted to tell you, and I think it might interest you.'

Sébastien glances up at her as he puts another helping on his plate. 'What is it?'

'When I was in London for the conference, there was a lecture about horses also. This woman, Gillian … I forgot her last name now, she talked about the strain horses are under when racing, or jumping.' Cécile looks at her father. 'I think many horse owners don't have a clue what's going on *inside* a horse. They only seem to be in it for the money.'

'Not always, Cécile. Take your grandfather, he always puts the welfare of the horses first,' Sébastien says in a defensive tone.

'True, but he might just be an exception. Anyway, she gave tips on how to appropriately train horses to diminish stress and strain on horses' joints. I mean, a correct way of riding, and a good posture of the rider – '

'That's the first thing a good trainer looks for, that the jockey sits well in the saddle,' Sébastien interjects.

'I'm sure they do, but do all trainers know?' is Cécile's reply. 'There are so many horses that get injured.'

Sébastien does not allow his true thoughts to be known, but he cannot help but determine that despite his daughter's aversion to horses, she has made an effort to find out more about them.

'Papa? Do you want to hear more?'

'Of course.'

'She talked about the best way to strengthen horses' muscles to reduce injuries,' Cécile says between two bites. 'So, she brought in her horse where she'd *painted* the skeleton on, and the muscle groups – '

'She put paint on a horse?' Sébastien finds that hard to believe.

Cécile now has Thomas's attention as well. 'Paint on a horse!' His childlike laugh echoes through the yard. His grandfather too, can't suppress a smile, if it were only for Thomas's infectious laughter.

'Papa! Do you want to hear it or not?'

'Of course, Cécile.' But his daughter looks at him critically.

'Please continue.'

' … She used all different colours on the horse's body, so that people would know where muscles and bones are *inside* a horse. That was what it was called.'

'Called what?'

'Horses Inside Out. I still kept a leaflet. You can have it if you want.'

Sébastien had no idea that his daughter would be interested in equine issues, and it warms his heart that she was mindful of her father's interests.

'I found it fascinating,' Cécile says. 'I'd never seen anything like that. It was all about understanding the anatomy and biomechanics of a horse to help improve training techniques.'

Her father shares her interest in the subject. 'You should tell your grandfather about this. It would really interest him. Just, don't mention the paint.' The last remark makes Thomas laugh again in his high-pitched voice.

'You, bed,' Cécile says.

'I'll take him,' Sébastien offers. 'Then *I* can tell you a nice horse story,' he tells his grandson while winking at his daughter at the same time.

A few days later, Sébastien finds his daughter at the kitchen table working on her laptop. 'Morning, Cécile,' and he strokes her hair. 'Where's Thomas? He wasn't in his room.'

'Where do you think? He's helping Julien in the stables.'

Sébastien notices Cécile has made sure that breakfast is ready, and the coffee is percolating on the counter. He pours himself a cup, then glances over his daughter's shoulder.

'Have you had your breakfast?' he wonders.

'Yes, we're fine. Papa, I hope you don't mind, but I'm trying to build you a website.'

'A website? What would I do with a website?'

'For your business, Papa. Everybody has a website nowadays.' She focusses on the screen and clicks on a few icons. 'It would be good to upload a few photos, too, so your customers can see what Les Jonquières looks like.'

His daughter keeps amazing him. He had no idea what a bright and independent young woman she had become. He sits down opposite her. 'I will take a few photos,' he says with a smile. 'And then, I'll go over to Fontenelle. On horseback. Would you like to come?'

The look on her face tells Sébastien that a ride on a horse is not something she had in mind.

'I hear your cousin Madeleine is starting to feel bored at La Fontenelle, missing her friends.'

'We've planned to go to Nice, shopping, a little later,' Cécile replies. 'Now, what do you think?' She turns the computer screen his way, clicks on an icon and up pops the home page. 'And in this section, you can upload some photos, and here's how much you charge.'

Sébastien is impressed. 'Thank you, Cécile. I never thought of a website.'

'Do you like the horsey theme?' Cécile asks.

Sébastien smiles. 'Yes, Cécile. I think the horsey theme is a great idea.' They look at each other, and Sébastien feels the unbroken connection they have, a connection that has always been there. Even the lost years have not changed that. The recollection of how he perceived the bond he had with his daughter all those years, has now faded into nothingness.

'There's something comforting about returning to home soil, Papa,' his daughter observes.

~.~.~.~.~

If you enjoyed reading this book then a review in your favourite online store would be much appreciated as it will help others to discover the story. Thank you!

~.~

You can join the Readers List here and get your free Ebook: https://cmuntjewerf.com/

List of French → English Words:

Bonjour = Hello, good morning, good afternoon

Jeune Homme (horse's name) = Young Man, later referred to as *Vieil Homme* = Old Man

chéri = darling

Monsieur = Mr, Sir

Clinique vétérinaire = Veterinary clinic

à gauche = to the left

vaurien = rascal

Bien = good, all right

Merci beaucoup = thank you very much

eau minérale = mineral water

Mais non! = But, no!

Jouets = games, toys

Oui, mon vieux. = Yes, my old friend.

Demain = tomorrow

Patron = boss, chief

Mon Dieu! = Good heavens! My God!

Merci. Merci bien = thank you

Grand-mère = grandmother, nannie

Grand-père = grandfather, granddad

bon apétit = Enjoy your meal.

émeutier = rioter

une auto = a car

arrière-grand-père = great-grandfather

arrière-grand-mère = great-grandmother

Quoi? = What?

Un secret = a secret

Ça ne fait rien = it doesn't matter

Marchand de bois = Wood trader

Mais oui! = That's right! Of Course!

Maman = mama

Messieurs = Gentlemen

Restez lá = stay here

Métèque (the large white dog's name) = stranger,

wanderer, foreigner

Coiffeur = hairdresser, stylist

parcour = course, training track, route to be covered

Monseigneur = When Sébastien was young, this was the name of one of Pierre's best horses who won many races.

D'accord = Okay

hein = huh, hey

Drôle d'odeur = funny smell

Police Municipale = local police

Zut alors = Shucks!

Retour à la case départ = Back to square one

Zut = heck, drat

Bien sûr = of course, obviously

Merci mon copain = thank you my friend

Lycée = secondary school, lyceum

Carrière = Sandy training circle

Là-bas = Over there

s'il te plaît = please

Allo = Hello

'*Ce qui se passe là* ... ' = What happens there? What's going on there?

Allez, on y vas! = Come on, let's go!

copain = buddy, pal, friend

premiers secours = First Aid, Emergency Services

le petit-déjeuner = breakfast

déjeuner = lunch

Milton Keynes UK
Ingram Content Group UK Ltd.
UKHW021727070624
443905UK00029B/312